CONNECTION IN TIME

THE UNSEEN THREADS OF FATE BETWEEN TWO HEARTS

MOHAMED YASIN

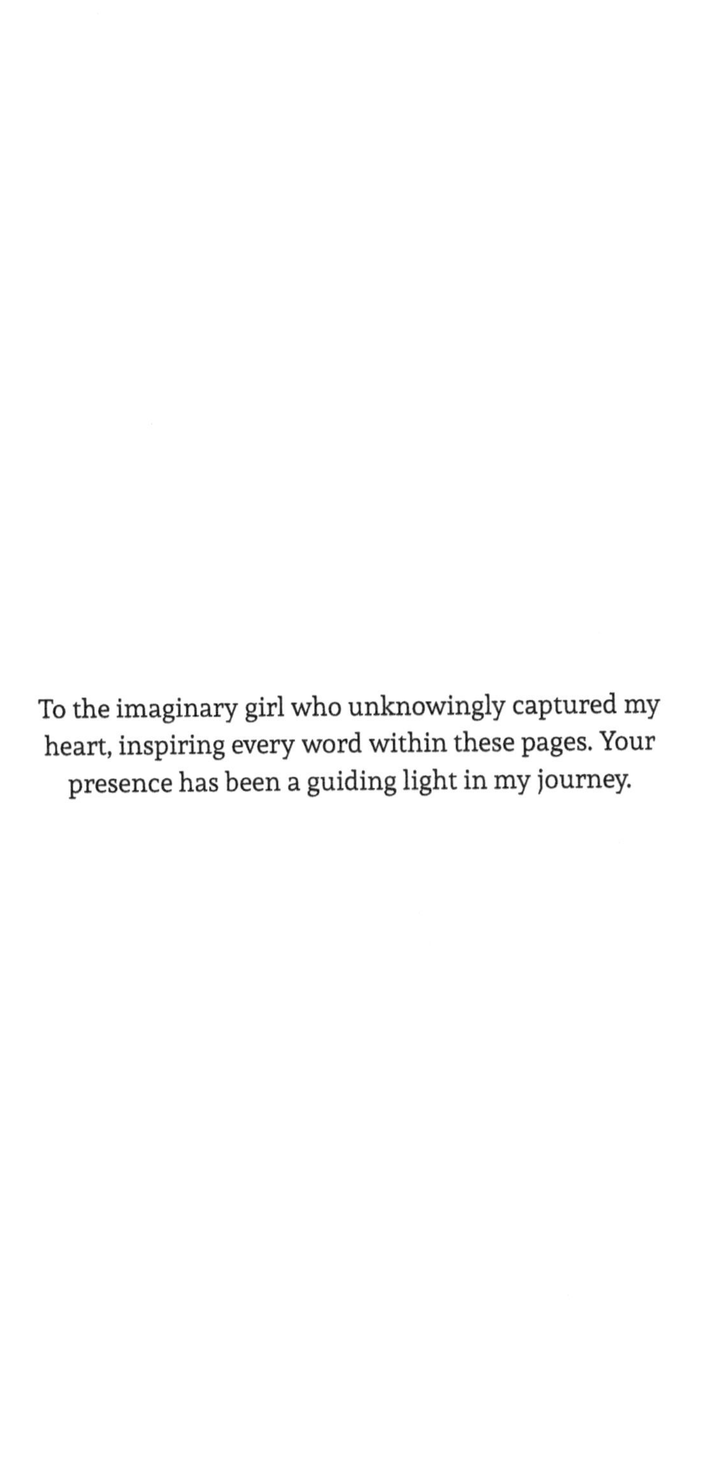

To the imaginary girl who unknowingly captured my heart, inspiring every word within these pages. Your presence has been a guiding light in my journey.

Contents

Contents

Preface

Writing "Connection in Time" has been a deeply personal journey for me. It started with a fleeting encounter that lingered in my mind for years, inspiring me to explore the intricate dance of emotions that comes with unspoken feelings and missed opportunities. This novel is an exploration of love, fate, and the mysterious threads that bind our lives together.

As I crafted this story, I found myself reflecting on the moments in my own life where connections were made and lost, and how those experiences shape who we are. I hope that readers will find themselves resonating with the characters and their struggles, perhaps seeing reflections of their own experiences in their journeys.

The road to writing this book was not without its challenges. There were days of self-doubt and uncertainty, but with the support of my family, friends, and fellow writers, I was able to push through. Each page brought me closer to understanding the characters I created and the story I wanted to tell.

This book is for anyone who has ever experienced the thrill of a connection, the pain of longing, and the hope that maybe, just maybe, fate has more in store for us. I invite you to join me in this exploration of love and destiny, and I hope you find as much joy in reading it as I found in writing it.

Thank you for embarking on this journey with me.

Acknowledgements

I would like to express my heartfelt gratitude to everyone who supported me throughout the journey of writing this novel. To my family and friends, thank you for your unwavering encouragement and belief in my vision. Your support has been invaluable.

I also want to acknowledge the inspiring authors and stories that fueled my imagination and passion for writing. Each page I read spurred my creativity and pushed me to keep writing.

Lastly, a huge thank you to anyone who has ever shared a story with me or offered a kind word; your influence has left a mark on my heart and my work.

Prologue

In a world bustling with noise and chaos, moments can slip by unnoticed, hidden in the folds of everyday life. It's the fleeting glances, the accidental brushes of shoulders, and the unsaid words that often carry the most weight. For him, it was a day like any other—filled with the mundane worries of assignments and deadlines—until it wasn't.

It all began at a college competition, where bright minds gathered to showcase their talents. He was just a boy then, brimming with dreams but shadowed by self-doubt. That day, he stepped into an unfamiliar auditorium, unaware that a single glance would change the course of his life. She entered like a breath of fresh air, effortlessly drawing him in with her laughter and grace. Though they exchanged no words, in that brief moment, she ignited something within him—a spark that would linger long after the day had ended.

Years passed, and the boy transformed into a man, carrying the memory of that encounter like a cherished secret. Fate, however, had a way of intertwining their paths once more. Now, they find themselves working side by side in the same office, both unaware of the invisible thread connecting their pasts. The weight of unspoken feelings hangs heavy in the air, as he grapples with the fear of revealing his heart.

As memories resurface and the mundane turns into the extraordinary, he begins to wonder: is this the second chance he never knew he wanted? Or is it simply a reminder of what could have been? In the silent spaces between their interactions, he embarks on a journey to unravel the mysterious forces that bind their lives together—a journey that will challenge his understanding of love, fate, and the significance of moments that shape us.

This is a story of one-sided love and the delicate dance of connections that can transcend time. In a world where everything feels transient, will he muster the courage to bridge the distance between them? Or will he remain forever tethered to a dream of what might have been?

1
Beginning of Connection

The sun was barely up when Sai's college bus pulled into the campus grounds of their competitors. As a second-year engineering student, Sai had been eagerly awaiting this day for weeks. It was his first time representing the college in an intercollegiate technical competition, a prestigious event that many of his seniors had spoken highly of. But despite the excitement, as the bus rolled past the modest entrance of the college, Sai's enthusiasm began to falter.

The college seemed ordinary. There were no banners or colorful decorations to mark the event, no buzz of excitement in the air. The gates, which carried the name of the institution in bold, sturdy letters, were flanked by neat hedges, but it lacked the grandeur he had imagined. The feeling of anticipation was still there, but it was tempered by a growing nervousness, one he couldn't quite explain. Perhaps it was the weight of representing his college or the fear of not living up to the expectations he'd placed on himself.

As the bus doors opened, the slight breeze carried with it the scent of freshly watered grass. Sai stepped out, adjusting the straps of his backpack as he took in the surroundings.

The campus, though simple, had an understated beauty. Tall trees provided shade, and the neatly manicured lawns gave a sense of calm, almost as if this place was built to let students escape the usual chaos of city life. The simplicity soothed his nerves a little, but it wasn't enough to completely erase the unease that had settled in his chest.

At the registration desk, Sai found himself standing behind a small crowd of participants from different colleges, all waiting to sign in. The girls managing the desk were friendly, their faces lit up with warm smiles as they processed the registrations. One of them, her hair falling in loose waves over her shoulder, asked for his name. There was a calm confidence in her voice, which oddly put him at ease.

Sai handed over his ID card, and she swiftly noted down his details before handing him a welcome kit. "Good luck!" she said, her smile lingering for a moment before she turned to the next participant. He nodded his thanks, clutching the kit in his hands as he made his way towards the auditorium, feeling a bit lighter now.

The auditorium was already filling up by the time Sai found a seat. The stage at the front was being prepped for the opening ceremony, and the sound of conversations echoed around the room. There were students from various colleges, some chatting excitedly, others quietly revising notes. But Sai couldn't focus on the lively atmosphere. His thoughts were elsewhere, his mind clouded by doubt. Am I ready for this? What if I mess up?

The event kicked off with the usual fanfare—introductions, speeches, and an explanation of the rules. But Sai's attention drifted. The competitions themselves didn't hold his interest the way he had hoped. His heart wasn't in it, and he found himself just going through the motions. Every now and then, he would glance around the room, as if searching for something or someone to break the monotony.

And then, she appeared.

At first, she was just part of the crowd—a girl walking down the aisle with a group of friends, laughing at something one of them had said. But there was something about her that caught Sai's eye. It wasn't just her appearance, though she was undeniably striking. It was the way she carried herself, with an effortless grace that set her apart. She didn't seem to notice the attention she garnered as she moved through the room, her laughter soft but clear, her presence magnetic.

Sai's gaze followed her as she took a seat a few rows ahead. There was a strange pull he felt toward her, a connection he couldn't quite explain. His heart, which had been weighed down with nervousness and doubt all morning, suddenly felt lighter. She didn't do anything out of the ordinary—she simply sat with her friends, engaged in conversation—but to Sai, she was the most captivating person in the room.

The rest of the day passed in a blur. Sai participated in the competitions, but his mind was elsewhere, fixated on the girl he had spotted earlier. He didn't know her name, didn't know anything about her, but she had made an indelible mark on him. He found himself scanning the crowd during breaks, hoping for another glimpse of her.

At lunch, he picked at his food, too distracted to eat. His friends were discussing strategies for the next round of the competition, but Sai wasn't paying attention. His thoughts kept drifting back to the girl with the infectious laughter and the effortless charm. He couldn't understand why he felt so drawn to her. It wasn't like him to get distracted, especially over someone he didn't know. But something about her presence had shifted something inside him.

As the day wore on, Sai grew more frustrated with himself. He was here to compete, to make his college proud, but instead, his mind was consumed by thoughts of a girl he hadn't even spoken to. He felt foolish, but he couldn't shake the feeling that she was somehow important.

By the time the final round of the competition rolled around, Sai had resigned himself to the fact that he wouldn't see her again. The event was wrapping up, and soon he would be back on the bus, heading home. But just as he was about to leave the auditorium, he spotted her again. She was standing by the exit, chatting with a friend, her smile as radiant as ever.

For a brief moment, their eyes met. Sai's heart skipped a beat. It was just a fleeting glance, but in that instant, something changed. He didn't know what it was, but he felt a spark, a connection that he couldn't ignore. And just like that, she was gone, disappearing into the crowd as quickly as she had appeared.

As Sai boarded the bus to head back to his college, he felt a strange mix of emotions. He hadn't spoken to her, hadn't learned her name, but the memory of that brief encounter stayed with him. She was a stranger, yet she had stirred something in him that he couldn't explain.

That night, as he lay in bed, her face lingered in his thoughts. He didn't know why, but he had a feeling that this wasn't the end. Something told him that their paths would cross again, and when they did, he would be ready.

Little did he know, that brief moment of connection would change the course of his life in ways he couldn't yet imagine.

2
The Stirring of Something New

The days after the competition drifted by in a strange haze, yet for Sai, something had fundamentally shifted. Life, on the surface, carried on as usual—lectures, assignments, project deadlines—but his mind was elsewhere, constantly circling back to the girl he had seen. He didn't even know her name, but her face stayed with him like an imprint, a silhouette that would reappear when he least expected it.

Sai wasn't the kind of person who got easily distracted. In fact, he had always prided himself on being focused and diligent, traits that had earned him top marks and the reputation of being a serious student. His world had always been predictable, neatly divided into subjects and responsibilities, free from any emotional entanglements. He had friends, sure, but not the kind that weighed heavily on his heart or mind. No girl had ever taken up space in his thoughts. Until now.

But this was different. This was... consuming.

For the first time in his life, Sai found himself unable to focus, his thoughts constantly drifting back to her. He couldn't help but feel a bit foolish—he hadn't even spoken to her, hadn't exchanged more than a fleeting glance in her direction. And yet, the memory of her smile, the sound of her laughter, the way she had moved through the crowd as if unaware of the effect she had on him, all lingered in his mind like a melody that wouldn't stop playing.

It was unsettling. He had never felt like this before. Love, crushes, or whatever these feelings were, had always been abstract concepts to Sai—things that happened in movies or to other people, but not to him. He had always assumed he was too practical for such distractions, too focused on his goals to be derailed by feelings. But now, here he was, unable to think about anything else.

He tried to brush it off. "It's just a phase," he told himself. "You'll forget her in a week." But deep down, he knew that wasn't true. There was something about this girl, something intangible, that had lodged itself in his mind and refused to leave. No matter how hard he tried to distract himself with studies or his usual routine, the thought of her always crept back in.

His friends noticed the change in him. "You've been quiet lately," one of them commented during lunch, poking at his plate. Sai barely touched his food, lost in his thoughts.

"Yeah, you seem out of it, man," another chimed in, looking at him curiously. "Everything okay?"

Sai forced a smile, shaking his head as if to clear away the fog in his mind. "Yeah, just a lot on my plate. You know, assignments and stuff."

But his friends weren't convinced. They exchanged glances, but thankfully, they didn't push him further. Sai wasn't ready to explain what he couldn't even fully understand himself. How could he tell them that a girl he'd never spoken to had taken over his thoughts? It sounded ridiculous, even to him.

That night, Sai lay in bed, staring up at the ceiling. The quiet of his room felt suffocating, pressing in on him as his mind replayed every moment from the competition—the way she had walked in with her friends, her easy laughter, the warmth in her eyes when she smiled. He wondered what her name was, what her voice sounded like in a real conversation. Did she notice him that day? Or was he just another face in the crowd to her?

He knew it was pointless to dwell on it. She was probably long gone, back to her own world, unaware of the effect she had left behind. But Sai couldn't help it. For someone who had never felt this kind of pull before, it was like discovering a new emotion altogether—a mix of curiosity, longing, and a strange sense of excitement that he hadn't anticipated.

The feelings were alien to him, unfamiliar in a way that was both thrilling and terrifying. He wasn't used to this kind of vulnerability, this sense of being out of control. He had always been the one steering his life, making plans and following them through, but now he found himself caught in a current he couldn't quite navigate.

And yet, despite the confusion, there was a part of him that didn't want to let go. For the first time in a long time, Sai felt alive in a way he hadn't before. It was as if something had awakened inside him, something he hadn't even known was missing.

Sleep eluded him that night, as it had every night since the competition. And though he knew it was futile, he couldn't help but wonder—would he ever see her again? Would fate be kind enough to let their paths cross once more?

As the city outside his window slowly quieted down, Sai felt a strange sense of anticipation, as if the universe was waiting for something to unfold. He didn't know what that something was, but deep down, he hoped it involved her.

Days turned into weeks, and though the routine of college life resumed, Sai couldn't shake the lingering thoughts of her. It was like living in two worlds—one where he kept up appearances, attending classes, discussing projects with his peers, and another where his mind wandered back to that fleeting moment in the auditorium. Every time he caught himself drifting, he felt a pang of frustration. He wasn't used to being distracted like this, especially over something so intangible.

His friends, oblivious to the storm brewing inside him, carried on as normal, teasing him about assignments, upcoming tests, and group hangouts. But Sai remained distant, almost as if part of him was always elsewhere. The truth was, ever since that day, he had started seeing the world differently. Colors seemed more vivid, the chatter of classmates a little louder, and even the small, mundane things like walking through the campus took on a strange new significance.

One afternoon, while sitting in the library, Sai found himself absentmindedly sketching in his notebook. He wasn't much of an artist, but the pencil moved on its own, forming random lines and shapes that somehow ended up resembling her face. He stared at the rough sketch, shaking his head in disbelief. What was happening to him? He felt ridiculous, obsessing over a girl he hadn't even spoken to. Yet here he was, drawn to her image like a moth to a flame.

He tore the page from his notebook and crumpled it, stuffing it deep into his bag. "This is insane," he muttered to himself. How could someone he barely knew have such an effect on him? He tried to focus on his studies, but the effort was futile. His mind kept replaying that brief encounter—her laughter, the easy way she moved through the crowd, and the calm aura she carried with her.

It wasn't just physical attraction. Sai had seen beautiful girls before, but none had ever left such an imprint on him. There was something deeper, something unexplainable that had drawn him to her. He couldn't put it into words, but he felt it every time he closed his eyes and saw her face.

One evening, after another long day of classes, Sai decided to take a walk around the campus. The sun was setting, casting a soft golden light over the buildings and pathways. It was quiet, the usual hustle and bustle of students replaced by the occasional rustling of leaves and the distant hum of traffic. As he walked, his thoughts naturally drifted back to her. He wondered what her life was like. Did she have friends who knew her better than anyone else? Did she have dreams, ambitions, worries that kept her up at night?

He felt a strange sense of curiosity growing inside him—a desire to know more, to understand the person behind that captivating presence. And yet, he was fully aware of how unrealistic this all was. She was probably living her life, unaware that she had left such a mark on him. Maybe she had already forgotten the competition, forgotten the crowd of strangers she had been part of. For all Sai knew, she had moved on, while he was stuck in this strange loop of feelings and thoughts that wouldn't let him go.

His steps slowed as he reached the edge of the campus, where the road led into the city. The sounds of honking cars and bustling pedestrians began to mix with the fading quiet of the evening, but Sai didn't feel like going back yet. He leaned against a nearby wall, staring out at the skyline, lost in thought.

It wasn't just about her, he realized. It was about what she represented—something new, something he had never experienced before. His life had been simple, straightforward, focused on his studies and his future. But now, there was this unexpected detour, this feeling of uncertainty that both excited and terrified him.

Sai wasn't used to uncertainty. He liked having a plan, knowing where he was headed. But with her, there were no plans, no clear path forward. It was all a mystery—a beautiful, confusing mystery that he couldn't help but be drawn to.

As the evening wore on, he finally decided to head back to his dorm. The campus was quieter now, the lights from the buildings casting long shadows across the ground. But as Sai walked back, he couldn't help but feel a sense of anticipation growing inside him. He didn't know what the future held, but for the first time in his life, he was okay with that. There was something thrilling about the unknown, about the possibility of something more.

He glanced up at the stars that had begun to twinkle in the darkening sky, a faint smile tugging at the corners of his lips. Maybe he would see her again, maybe not. But for now, just the thought of her was enough to keep him moving forward, to keep him hopeful.

As he reached his dorm room and unlocked the door, Sai couldn't shake the feeling that this was just the beginning of something. What that something was, he didn't know yet. But whatever it was, he was ready to find out.

3

The Cricket Match

A year had passed since that unforgettable moment in the auditorium, and Sai's life had fallen into a steady rhythm. Days turned into weeks, and college life consumed him—lectures, assignments, the occasional hangout with friends. But despite the busy schedule, his thoughts often drifted back to her, the girl from the competition. He hadn't seen her since, but the memory of her lingered like a shadow in his mind.

One afternoon, while lounging in the common room, a senior burst in, brimming with excitement.

"Hey, everyone! We're putting together a team for the inter-college cricket tournament! We need players!" he shouted, waving a colorful poster in the air.

Sai barely looked up. Cricket had never been his thing, and the idea of spending time in practice sessions felt more like a burden than a chance to unwind. He sighed, leaning back in his chair, disinterested.

"Nah, not for me," he muttered, hoping to be left out of the conversation.

"C'mon, Sai! This is your chance to represent our college!" the senior urged.

"Yeah, you guys go ahead. I'll focus on my studies," Sai said dismissively, waving his hand as if to brush off the idea.

The senior shrugged and turned to leave, but Sai's curiosity was piqued when he caught a glimpse of the poster. Something felt familiar. He stood up and grabbed it, his eyes scanning the details—and then it hit him. The tournament was to be held at her college.

Suddenly, the idea of playing didn't seem so bad after all. "Wait," he called after the senior. "Is it too late to join the team?"

The senior raised an eyebrow, surprised at Sai's change of heart. "You sure? I thought you weren't interested?"

Sai smirked. "I changed my mind. I've got a good reason now."

The senior, amused, handed him the registration form. "Fine, but don't bail on us halfway through!"

That night, Sai lay awake in bed, thinking of her. What were the chances that he might see her again? His heart raced at the thought, and he barely slept as visions of her face filled his mind. The next morning, he was up before the sun, anticipation buzzing through him. He dressed quickly in a casual outfit, hoping he might bump into her during the tournament.

As the bus approached her college, Sai stared out the window, his excitement building. The campus looked just as he remembered—lush greenery surrounding the pathways, students milling about, the air filled with laughter. He scanned the crowd, looking for a familiar face, but she was nowhere to be seen.

The match began, but Sai found it impossible to focus. His eyes kept wandering to the crowd, searching for her. His teammates teased him about his distracted behavior, but he brushed it off, telling them it was nerves.

By lunchtime, Sai was exhausted, not from the game, but from the constant anticipation. He slumped onto a bench under a large tree, his hope dwindling with each passing minute. As he stared into the distance, wondering if he'd ever see her again, a voice called out behind him.

"Hey, Chinese!"

Startled, Sai turned his head, irritated at the sound of the nickname. But then his irritation melted away as his eyes landed on her. She was walking with a group of friends, her laughter ringing in the air. She was just as he remembered—radiant and effortless. And once she crossed then he slowly telling himself Chinese with a mild smile.

Today, she was wearing a white salwar, the color complimenting her glowing skin. A small pendant shaped like a delicate dollar hung from her neck, shimmering in the sunlight. But it wasn't just the pendant that caught his attention—it was the way she moved, her smile bright and genuine, her hair flowing in the breeze. There was something about her that seemed almost ethereal, as if she carried a light with her wherever she went.

Sai's breath caught in his throat. She was beautiful in a way that made his chest tighten. Her features were soft, her eyes expressive and filled with warmth. Her smile was gentle, yet captivating, and for the first time, Sai realized just how rare that smile was. He had seen her smile with her friends before, but this time, it felt different—personal, as if that smile was meant for him.

As she passed by, completely unaware of his presence, Sai felt a pang of longing. It was almost as if the universe had placed her in front of him and then cruelly pulled her away again.

Suddenly, one of her friends nudged her, whispering something that made her glance in Sai's direction. Their eyes met for a brief moment, and Sai's heart skipped a beat. She looked at him—just a quick glance—but then, something surprising happened. She smiled.

Not the kind of smile she gave her friends or the polite one she flashed to strangers. No, this smile felt different. It was softer, more personal. Sai felt a rush of warmth as if that brief smile had been meant just for him. For the first time, he felt like he owned a piece of her world, even if it was just a fleeting moment.

She turned back to her friends, continuing their conversation as they walked away, but Sai remained frozen, replaying that smile in his mind. His pulse quickened, and he realized that seeing her like this—so close yet still distant—only made his feelings for her grow stronger.

Sai leaned back against the tree, closing his eyes for a moment. She was so close now, not just in his memories or his imagination, but here, in front of him, within reach. He didn't know how, but he had to find a way to talk to her, to bridge the gap between them.

The afternoon passed in a blur. Sai barely noticed the second half of the cricket match, his mind too preoccupied with thoughts of her. He had always admired her from afar, but today felt different. She had smiled at him, and that single moment had made everything feel possible.

By the time the sun began to set, Sai's heart was still racing. The memory of her white salwar, her delicate pendant, and that unforgettable smile stayed with him as they boarded the bus back to his college. He sat by the window, lost in thought, wondering when he might see her again.

He didn't know it yet, but that brief encounter would mark the beginning of something new. Sai couldn't wait for the next opportunity to be near her, to speak with her, to see if that smile was truly meant for him.

4

His World

College life had a predictable rhythm for Sai. The days passed in a blend of lectures, assignments, and casual banter with his friends, but amidst it all, he preferred staying slightly on the edge—observing rather than leading. Sai wasn't one to chase the limelight, and his quiet nature sometimes made people think he was distant. But those who spent time with him knew that behind his composed exterior lay a thoughtful, curious mind that soaked in the world around him.

In his second year of engineering, Sai was pursuing electronics, a field that both fascinated and challenged him. He wasn't the top of his class, but he took pride in the understanding he had of the subject, never satisfied with just memorizing formulas or chasing grades. He preferred solving problems deeply, taking his time to absorb concepts fully.

Despite his reserved nature, Sai had a wide circle of friends, not just in his own electronics department but also in the computer science, mechanical, and petroleum engineering departments. He had a way of connecting with people across disciplines—some drawn by his quiet wisdom, others by his dry sense of humor that appeared when least expected. Even among seniors, both in his department and others, Sai was well-respected, often sought out for advice or a calm perspective.

Most of Sai's afternoons were spent with his core group of friends—Raj, Adi, and Neha. They'd gather at the canteen, their usual meeting spot after the chaos of morning lectures, sharing plates of samosas and chai while laughing about the day's events. Raj was the loudest of the group, always pulling some stunt or cracking a joke, while Adi was the tech geek, always up to date with the latest trends in gadgets. Neha, the calmest of the trio, had a way of balancing them out, offering advice when things got out of hand.

But even as Sai laughed along with his friends, there was a part of him that felt disconnected. Not from them, but from the larger experience of college life. While his friends thrived on the energy of social events, parties, and the thrill of competition, Sai found more comfort in solitude. He liked wandering around the quieter corners of campus—whether it was sitting by the lake, where the sunlight danced on the water, or walking through empty hallways when most students had left for the day.

Evenings were a different story. After college, Sai often met up with his friends from other departments—guys from computer science, mechanical engineering, and even a few from petroleum. They'd hang out by the ground, talking about everything from upcoming tests to life outside the classroom, sometimes joining in for a casual game of soccer or heading to the gym. For Sai, these moments were more than just unwinding; they were a way of staying connected without the noise of large social circles. The ground became a place where Sai could switch off the academic part of his brain and just be, whether running on the soccer field or lifting weights at the gym.

Dinner was often a continuation of this routine, with Sai heading to the mess hall or a small nearby restaurant with his friends, laughing over simple conversations, swapping stories of the day's events. Despite being quiet, Sai's presence in these moments was never overlooked. His friends valued his thoughtful input, and his ability to listen made them feel understood.

But behind it all—his interactions, his studies, and his quiet moments—there was something else that lingered in his mind. It wasn't something he spoke about, not even to his closest friends. He couldn't shake the image of her from his thoughts. He would see her in passing on campus sometimes, though he never let on that he noticed. There was something about those brief moments when he saw her—the way she moved through the crowd, the quiet grace with which she carried herself—that struck him deeply.

He remembered the time he had first seen her, the fleeting moments of connection in the auditorium, and more recently at the cricket match. These memories, as distant as they felt, clung to him. Sai wasn't sure what to make of it. He wasn't the type to get swept up in grand romantic notions, but there was something about her that stayed with him, and he couldn't quite explain why.

Despite spending most evenings with his friends, either on the field or at the gym, these thoughts of her would sneak in during the quieter moments—when he was alone, walking back to his hostel under the dim lights, or lying in bed at night, listening to the distant hum of the city outside.

His days followed a steady pattern—classes, friends, evening games, and quiet moments. And yet, as ordinary as his routine seemed, Sai knew that something within him had shifted. Even as he sat with his friends, bantered with Raj, or helped Adi with his latest tech project, there was a part of him that was elsewhere. Somewhere far away, lingering on the thought of her.

5

The Struggle within

Sai had always been the quiet one. Ever since school, he had maintained a distance from girls, not because he disliked them, but because he simply never knew what to say. It wasn't that he was shy, but he found conversations with girls perplexing, often confusing, as if they spoke in a different language he couldn't quite decipher. His school days were a blur of books, classes, and football matches. Friendships had always been easier with boys who shared his interests—sports, studies, the casual banter that didn't require him to be anything more than himself.

College hadn't changed much of that. Sai was still the reserved one, the guy who listened more than he spoke, especially around girls. While his friends had started to develop easy camaraderie with girls from their classes and other departments, Sai never felt that pull. He was friendly, yes, but never close. He couldn't remember the last time he had held a conversation with a girl that went beyond polite pleasantries.

He often wondered if something was wrong with him, if this inability to form connections with girls was something he needed to work on. But every time he tried, his words would freeze in his throat, his thoughts racing too fast for him to string a coherent sentence together. So, he stuck to what was comfortable—his friends, his studies, his own quiet world.

But now, everything was different.

She had changed everything. Without even realizing it, she had flipped his world upside down. Ever since the day he had seen her in the auditorium during the competition, Sai couldn't stop thinking about her. It baffled him. Why her? Why now? He had spent years avoiding anything remotely romantic, yet here he was, day after day, caught in thoughts of her.

At first, he brushed it off, convinced that it was just a fleeting crush, something that would pass. But after seeing her again at the cricket match, the intensity of his feelings grew. Every time he closed his eyes, he saw her—her face, her walk, the way she carried herself with quiet grace. And it wasn't just when he was alone. She invaded his thoughts even when he was with his friends, laughing and joking with them. It was as if she had taken root in his mind, and no matter how hard he tried, he couldn't shake her presence.

He found himself lost in thought, questioning his own feelings. Why her? he asked himself over and over again. She was just another student, one of the hundreds he passed by every day. There was no reason for him to be so fixated on her. He barely even knew her. And yet, something about her had stirred something deep within him, something he didn't understand and wasn't sure he wanted to.

In his mind, he tried to rationalize it. She was just a girl. There was nothing special about her, at least nothing that should make him feel this way. He didn't even know her name. How could he be so captivated by someone he hadn't spoken to? And yet, despite his best efforts, every time he tried to push her out of his thoughts, she came back stronger, her image clearer, her presence more real.

It frustrated him to no end. Sai wasn't the type to get swept up in emotions. He was logical, grounded, always thinking things through before acting. But when it came to her, all of that flew out the window. His usual calm was replaced by a whirlwind of confusion and longing, a feeling he wasn't used to and didn't know how to handle.

He started avoiding places where he might run into her. The idea of seeing her again both thrilled and terrified him. Part of him longed for even a fleeting glance, while another part dreaded the intensity of his own emotions. He couldn't allow himself to fall deeper into this—whatever this was. It wasn't right, and he knew it. He didn't even know her, not really, and yet she had a hold on him that he couldn't explain.

Sai tried to distract himself with his routine—going to the gym, playing football with his friends, burying himself in his studies. He'd throw himself into conversations, laugh louder, joke more, but no matter what he did, she was always there, lurking in the corners of his mind. When he was happy, when he was sad, when he was simply bored—her image would flash before his eyes, unbidden, unwanted.

And the worst part was, he couldn't talk to anyone about it. His friends wouldn't understand. They'd laugh, tease him about having a crush, but this felt different. It wasn't a simple crush. It was something more consuming, more confusing. He didn't know how to put it into words, and so he kept it all bottled up inside, fighting a silent battle with himself.

Late at night, when the world was quiet, and he was alone in his room, the struggle intensified. His thoughts would drift back to her, replaying the moments he had seen her—the way her hair caught the light, the subtle way she smiled when talking to her friends. He would lie awake for hours, tossing and turning, trying to convince himself that it didn't matter. She didn't matter.

But every time he tried, she would come back, like a whisper in the back of his mind, soft but insistent.

One night, as he lay in bed, staring up at the ceiling, Sai made a decision. He couldn't do this anymore. He couldn't let her occupy so much of his thoughts. It wasn't healthy. He didn't even know her. He had to let go. Whatever this was, it wasn't real. It was just a fantasy, a projection of something he thought he wanted but didn't truly understand.

She doesn't matter, he told himself firmly. I need to move on. Focus on what's real—on my studies, my friends, my life. He repeated the words over and over in his mind, hoping that saying it enough times would make it true.

The next day, Sai woke up determined. He threw himself into his routine, blocking out every thought of her. It was hard—harder than he expected—but he was resolved. Every time her face flashed in his mind, he pushed it away, focusing on the present, on the things he could control. He wouldn't let himself fall any deeper into this. He couldn't.

But even as he tried to move on, a small part of him wondered if he was fighting a losing battle. Because no matter how hard he tried, no matter how strong his resolve, she was always there, just out of reach, lingering in the quiet corners of his mind.

6

Home and Challenge ahead

The semester had been dragging on, each day blending into the next as the weight of upcoming exams hung heavy in the air. It was the end of Sai's second year, and the pressure to perform well felt more intense than ever. Subjects had grown tougher, classes more demanding, and Sai found himself spending hours in the library, poring over textbooks and notes, trying to make sense of everything before the exams hit.

One subject, in particular, loomed large in his mind—Control Systems. For Sai, it had been a constant source of frustration throughout the semester. No matter how much he studied, the complex equations and abstract concepts refused to stick. His professor's explanations only seemed to make things more confusing, and each time he thought he had finally grasped an idea, another layer of complexity would appear, leaving him feeling lost all over again.

As the day of the Control Systems exam approached, Sai felt a familiar knot form in his stomach. He had done his best to prepare, but deep down, he knew it wasn't enough. The night before the exam, he sat in his room, staring blankly at his notes, trying to force the information into his mind. Sleep eluded him, his thoughts racing with anxiety about the test ahead. What if I fail? The question gnawed at him, but he pushed it away, reminding himself that worrying wouldn't help.

The morning of the exam arrived, and as Sai took his seat in the exam hall, his heart pounded in his chest. The paper was laid before him, and as he scanned the questions, a sinking feeling washed over him. Half of it felt foreign, as if he had never seen the material before. He did his best, scribbling down answers wherever he could, but when the exam finally ended, Sai knew it hadn't gone well.

Still, there was nothing more he could do. The semester had come to an end, and now it was time to head home for the holidays. After a grueling year, the thought of going back to his hometown felt like a much-needed escape. He hadn't been home in months, and the idea of spending time with his family and old friends was a welcome distraction from the academic struggles of the past few weeks.

Sai's journey home was peaceful. He boarded the train, a well-worn backpack slung over his shoulder, and settled into his seat by the window. As the train began to pull away from the station, he watched the familiar cityscape fade into the distance, replaced by sprawling fields and countryside. The rhythmic hum of the train's wheels against the tracks had always been calming for Sai, and he found himself relaxing for the first time in weeks.

As the journey stretched on, Sai's thoughts drifted to his hometown. It had been too long since he had walked those streets, too long since he had sat on the front porch of his family's house, listening to the familiar sounds of his neighborhood. The prospect of seeing his childhood friends again made him smile. They had all gone off to different colleges, but the bond they shared had never weakened. Every time they came home for holidays, it was as if no time had passed at all.

Hours later, the train pulled into the small station of his hometown. Sai stepped off the train, the warm, humid air immediately enveloping him. The familiar scent of his hometown—a mixture of the nearby sea breeze and the earthy smell of the soil—brought a flood of memories rushing back. He could almost see his younger self, running through the streets with his friends, carefree and full of energy.

At home, his family welcomed him with open arms. His mother fussed over him, asking about his studies, while his father gave him a knowing smile, already aware that Sai wasn't in the mood to talk about exams just yet. After dinner, he wandered through the old streets, meeting up with his childhood friends at their usual spot by the local tea stall. They were all in high spirits, laughing and joking, sharing stories about their time in college.

Two of his closest friends, Vinod and Arun, were also studying in the same college as Sai, though in different departments. They were in Computer Science and Mechanical Engineering, and their roll numbers placed them right next to Sai in most of the semester exams. As they sat around with their cups of steaming tea, they started discussing their exam experiences.

"I think I barely survived Control Systems," Sai admitted, rubbing the back of his neck.

Arun laughed. "Same here, man. That subject is a nightmare."

Vinod chimed in, "Our labs this semester were brutal. You should have seen the chaos during the final evaluations. People were scrambling to finish their programs."

Their conversations meandered from college struggles to random stories about their classmates, professors, and the occasional misadventures in their respective departments. Some of their friends from other colleges joined them later in the evening, sharing their own stories of difficult exams and strict professors.

Every evening during the holidays, they would gather at the same spot, sometimes going to the local beach when they felt like taking a break from their tea sessions. They caught up on everything—movies, sports, and life in general. On one of those days, they decided to go to a movie in town, a local action flick that had been the talk of the town for weeks. The theater was packed, the atmosphere electric with excitement. Sai found himself laughing along with his friends at the absurd plot twists, feeling the stress of the past few weeks slowly melt away.

But the holiday wasn't all fun and games. Sai couldn't completely shake the thought of his Control Systems exam. The more time he spent with his friends, the more he heard stories of their struggles with tough subjects and realized he wasn't alone. Still, the possibility of failing lingered at the back of his mind, casting a shadow over the otherwise joyful holiday.

After two weeks of relaxing and reconnecting with his roots, it was time for Sai to head back to college for his third year. The night before he left, he sat with his friends, all of them knowing that it would be months before they could hang out like this again. They promised to stay in touch, but Sai knew that college life had a way of making those promises harder to keep.

On the morning of his departure, Sai packed his bags and said goodbye to his family. His mother hugged him tightly, reminding him to focus on his studies, while his father gave him a gentle pat on the back, wishing him luck. As he boarded the train back to college, Sai felt a mix of emotions—excitement for the new semester ahead, but also a nagging sense of dread about his exam results.

The journey back to college felt different from the one coming home. The landscape outside the window, though the same, seemed less vibrant, and Sai found himself lost in thought as the train sped along. The joy of the holidays had given way to the reality of what awaited him back at college.

When he arrived, the campus was abuzz with students returning from their holidays, each of them dragging suitcases and exchanging stories of their time away. Sai felt the weight of the new semester settle on his shoulders as he made his way to his dorm room. The familiar routine quickly kicked in—unpacking, setting up his books, and getting back into the rhythm of college life.

A week into the new semester, the results for the previous exams were posted. Sai's heart raced as he approached the notice board, scanning the list of names and marks. When his eyes landed on his result for Control Systems, his heart sank. He had failed.

The realization hit him hard. He had expected it, sure, but seeing the failure in black and white made it feel all the more real. For the rest of the day, Sai walked around in a daze, trying to process the failure. His friends, Vinod and Arun, tried to cheer him up, reminding him that they all had struggled and that this was just a temporary setback. But no matter what they said, Sai couldn't shake the feeling of disappointment.

It wasn't just about failing the subject—it was about what it represented. Control Systems was a hurdle he couldn't overcome, and now, in his third year, that failure weighed heavily on his mind. He knew he would have to retake the exam, and the thought of going through all that stress again made him feel exhausted.

But Sai wasn't one to give up easily. As the days passed, he started to accept the failure as part of his journey. It wasn't the end, just a bump in the road. With the support of his friends and a renewed determination, Sai set his sights on mastering the subject, knowing that this time, he wouldn't let it defeat him.

7
A Victory in Numbers

The first day of the new semester had arrived, and as Sai walked across the sunlit courtyard of the college, a mixture of emotions churned inside him. It was the day results for the 4th semester were posted. Although he had been prepared for what was coming, the weight of failing Control Systems still lingered heavily on his shoulders. He knew the retest was inevitable, and the thought gnawed at him, despite his attempts to remain positive.

But there was also another side to the day, a small ray of hope that kept the weight from becoming unbearable. Sai had always been good at Mathematics. In fact, it was one of the few subjects that had felt like second nature to him, a place where his mind seemed to naturally thrive. And today, he had pinned his hopes on the mathematics results. For months, he had been driven by a challenge, one that came from his deep bond with someone who was more than just a professor—Ms. Rekha, his Mathematics teacher.

Ms. Rekha was unlike any other professor in the college. She was strong, assertive, and fiercely dedicated to her subject. A woman in her early forties, with a sharp intellect and an even sharper tongue, she had earned the respect of both students and faculty. It was her firmness and unwavering passion for Mathematics that drew Sai to her from the very first class. She wasn't just a teacher, she was a force of nature—a mentor who pushed her students to their limits.

Yet, behind her stern exterior, Sai had found something softer. Over time, he had become one of her favorite students. Ms. Rekha would often share stories of her own college days, where she had been a bright student but had never achieved the top grades she had always longed for. For the past five years, none of her students had managed to score an O grade in Mathematics—a perfect grade that required precision, hard work, and a mastery of the subject. This fact had weighed heavily on her, though she never openly admitted it.

Sai, on the other hand, had seen the frustration in her eyes. He had heard the disappointment in her voice when she spoke of her students' potential and how close some of them had come to getting that top grade, only to fall short in the end. It was during one of their conversations, in the middle of his second year, that Sai made a decision—a promise, really. He would be the one to break the pattern. He would be the student to get that O grade for Ms. Rekha.

It hadn't been an easy road. The semester had been filled with endless study sessions, late nights, and countless hours spent solving equations and proofs. Sai had poured over every problem, refusing to leave even the smallest detail unexamined. He knew the challenge he had taken on, and he wasn't going to let her down.

Ms. Rekha, in return, had been both supportive and demanding. She held extra tutoring sessions for him, challenging him with problems that pushed the boundaries of the syllabus. "I don't care if this is beyond your exams," she had told him during one particularly grueling session, "You should be able to solve anything I throw at you. That's how you'll earn your O grade."

The two of them had built a unique relationship—part mentor, part friend, part taskmaster. In the weeks leading up to the exams, Ms. Rekha had begun to feel confident in Sai's abilities, but there was always a small part of her that feared disappointment. *What if he fails like the others?* she had wondered silently, though she never voiced it.

And now, the day of reckoning had come.

As Sai reached the results board, a crowd of students had already gathered. He squeezed his way through the throng of excited and nervous classmates, his eyes scanning the list of names and numbers. He quickly found his name under the Mathematics column, and there it was—a bright O next to his marks.

He blinked, barely able to process it at first. *O grade. I did it.* A surge of pride swelled within him, momentarily overshadowing the sting of his failure in Control Systems. He had made a promise, and he had kept it.

Just as the realization settled in, a familiar voice interrupted his thoughts. "Sai!" He turned to see Ms. Rekha standing there, her face alight with pride. She wasn't the kind of woman who showed emotion easily, but today, she didn't hold back. She walked right up to him, her eyes shining with something like triumph, and before Sai could even speak, she extended her hand.

"You did it," she said, her voice uncharacteristically soft. "I knew you could."

Sai shook her hand, but the gesture quickly turned into a heartfelt hug—something neither of them had expected. Ms. Rekha stepped back, laughing lightly, as if surprised by her own reaction.

"I've waited five years for this," she admitted. "Five years, Sai. And you—" she shook her head, as if at a loss for words. "You're the one who finally broke the cycle."

Her praise made Sai's chest swell with pride. It wasn't just about the grade—it was about the respect they had for each other, the bond they had built through countless hours of hard work and determination. And that's when it happened—the moment Sai would remember forever. Ms. Rekha smiled, the kind of smile that could light up a room, and said, "You're the reason I still teach."

As word of Sai's achievement spread, professors from other departments started appearing at his classroom door. One by one, they congratulated him, their words echoing the pride that Ms. Rekha had already expressed. Even professors he barely knew were eager to shake his hand and wish him well. Sai had never been the type to seek attention, but in that moment, he felt like he had achieved something truly remarkable.

It wasn't about proving something to the world—it was about fulfilling a promise to someone who believed in him. And for the first time in a long while, Sai felt like he had truly made a difference.

That same week, Sai and his friends decided to celebrate Ms. Rekha's birthday. They planned a small surprise party on campus, something simple yet heartfelt. Sai had ordered a cake, and his friends had arranged for decorations in one of the quieter corners of the campus. When Ms. Rekha arrived, she was genuinely touched by the gesture.

As the group gathered around her, cutting the cake and sharing stories, Sai couldn't help but feel a deep sense of gratitude for the woman who had pushed him to achieve his best. It was a joyous occasion, filled with laughter and warmth, and Sai felt like he had gained more than just a grade—he had gained a mentor, a guide, and a lifelong friend.

But little did Sai know, this would be the last time he would see Ms. Rekha. Shortly after the semester began, she transferred to another college, leaving behind a legacy that Sai would carry with him for years to come.

The news of her departure hit Sai hard. He hadn't expected her to leave so suddenly, and there had been no proper goodbye. But as he stood in the classroom one last time, where they had spent so many hours working together, Sai realized something important—Ms. Rekha had given him everything he needed. Her influence would stay with him, guiding him through the challenges ahead.

And as Sai walked out of that classroom, he knew that the lessons he had learned from her were far more valuable than any grade could ever be.

8
A New Kind of Friendship

The second year of college brought with it an unexpected opportunity for Sai. One afternoon, while lounging with his friends in the campus canteen, he was summoned to the department office. A committee had been formed by the college to organize events, communicate information, and represent various departments for inter-college activities. Each class was asked to send a representative, and to Sai's surprise, he had been chosen to represent his class from the Electronics department.

It felt like an honor and a responsibility he wasn't quite prepared for. While he was usually comfortable working alone, this committee role would require regular interactions, meetings, and coordination. What made it even more interesting—and slightly intimidating—was that two other girls, one from the third year and another from the final year, had been selected alongside him to represent their department.

The first committee meeting was scheduled for Friday afternoon. Sai arrived at the appointed conference room, slightly anxious. As he stepped inside, his eyes immediately fell on Sofi, the final-year student from his department. She was seated with the third-year representative, a girl named Riya, who seemed more interested in checking her phone than the meeting ahead. Sofi, however, was something else entirely.

Sofi was, by far, one of the most popular girls in the college. She wasn't just known for her striking beauty but also for her warm and approachable nature. Her long, jet-black hair fell in loose waves around her shoulders, and her smile had a way of lighting up the room. She had sharp, almond-shaped eyes that held a kind of gentle confidence. Her skin was a warm, dusky hue, and she dressed with effortless style—never overly flashy but always graceful.

As Sai walked in, a few boys from other departments glanced enviously at him. They had been eyeing Sofi, hoping to catch her attention, but it was Sai who got to sit beside her at the committee table, purely by coincidence—or perhaps by fate. He took a seat, feeling the weight of all the attention in the room, especially the unspoken curiosity from his male peers.

Sofi noticed his slight discomfort and immediately broke the ice. "Hi, Sai, right?" she said with a smile. "I've heard about you. Welcome to the team."

Her voice was soft but steady, and her demeanor instantly put him at ease. It was clear why everyone admired her. Unlike the coldness or aloofness one might expect from someone so popular, Sofi exuded a genuine warmth that drew people in effortlessly.

For Sai, this was something completely new. In school, he had rarely spoken to girls. He was always the quiet one, keeping to himself and his close circle of friends. Even in college, he hadn't interacted much with his female classmates. Now, here he was, sitting with one of the most sought-after girls on campus, sharing responsibilities in a committee. It was a situation that left him feeling both excited and slightly nervous.

The weekly committee meetings became a regular part of Sai's schedule. Every Friday, they would gather in the same room to discuss upcoming events, important announcements, and any other tasks that needed to be communicated to their respective classes. Sofi always made sure to include Sai in the conversations, often turning to him for his input on decisions, making him feel like an equal partner rather than just a younger representative.

Meanwhile, Riya, the third-year girl, enjoyed teasing Sai whenever she got the chance. She wasn't mean-spirited about it, but there was a mischievous twinkle in her eye whenever she tried to get a reaction out of him. She would poke fun at how shy he seemed around girls, or how he didn't quite know how to handle all the attention Sofi was giving him. But Sofi never let the teasing go too far. If Riya pushed Sai too much, Sofi would step in with a gentle, yet firm, comment that stopped the teasing in its tracks.

Over time, Sai grew more comfortable around Sofi. He found himself looking forward to the committee meetings, not just for the work but for the time he got to spend with her. After the meetings, they often stayed back to discuss more details—though, more often than not, the conversations drifted into casual topics. They talked about their families, their plans after college, and shared funny stories about professors and classmates. Sofi would laugh at his jokes, and Sai found himself opening up in ways he never had before.

One Friday afternoon, after yet another meeting, Sofi turned to him with a playful grin. "You know, Sai, you're one of the few people who doesn't treat me like I'm some kind of celebrity around here."

Sai was caught off guard. "What do you mean?"

She laughed. "Come on, don't pretend you haven't noticed. All the boys in this college want to talk to me, hang out with me. It's like they're trying too hard. But with you—it feels natural. Like I'm just a regular person."

Sai didn't know what to say. He had noticed, of course. He had seen the way others flocked around her, but to him, Sofi was more than just her looks. She was kind, thoughtful, and easy to talk to. And for some reason, she had chosen to spend her time with him.

After the first few weeks, their interactions extended beyond the committee meetings. They began messaging each other on their phones, sharing memes, jokes, and random thoughts throughout the week. On weekends, they occasionally met up outside of campus, visiting cafes, going for walks, or just spending time together at the beach. Sometimes, Sofi would invite him for lunch during the week, and they would sit together, away from the rest of the committee, discussing college events and life in general.

There was a comfort in their bond that was hard for Sai to describe. Spending time with Sofi felt like stepping into a new world—a world where he wasn't just a shy boy who kept to himself. With her, he felt like he could be himself without any judgment. He even began calling her by her first name, something no other boy in college would dare to do.

Yet, despite the ease he felt around her, Sai couldn't help but be overwhelmed at times. This was the first time he had ever spent so much time with a girl. He would catch himself thinking about her long after their conversations ended, replaying moments in his head and wondering what it all meant. Was this just friendship? Or was there something more to the connection they shared?

One afternoon, after another committee meeting, Sai found himself sitting with Sofi in the campus garden. It was a quiet spot, away from the usual crowds, where they often retreated to talk in peace. Sofi was laughing at something Sai had said, her smile bright and genuine. As Sai watched her, he felt a strange warmth spread through him—a feeling he had never experienced before.

He wasn't sure what it was, but there was something about Sofi's presence that made everything feel lighter. She was the first girl he had truly spent time with, the first girl who had seen him for who he was without any expectations or pretenses. And while Sai knew that boys all over campus would have done anything to be in his shoes, he felt strangely lucky that Sofi had chosen him, without any effort on his part.

As the semester progressed, Sai and Sofi's bond only grew stronger. They continued to spend their lunch breaks together, sometimes alone, sometimes with other friends. Riya's teasing continued, but by now, it was all in good fun, and Sai had learned to take it in stride.

Looking back, Sai would always remember that year as the time when he first learned what it meant to truly connect with someone. Sofi had been more than just a popular girl or a senior mentor—she had been a friend, one who had opened his world in ways he hadn't expected.

And while their time together in the committee eventually came to an end, the memories of those afternoons, the laughter, and the conversations they shared stayed with him long after. Sofi had been his first real introduction to the world of friendship beyond the familiar, and though Sai never voiced it aloud, he knew deep down that their bond had changed him for the better.

9
Bonds Beyond the Classroom

Sai's college journey was marked by moments of unexpected friendships, guidance, and the strong bonds he built with some remarkable women who left a lasting impact on his life. Ms. Rekha, his strict yet supportive mathematics teacher, had been one such figure who had inspired him to achieve something greater in his academic life. Sofi, his senior and the first girl he ever really connected with, had opened a new chapter of camaraderie and friendship during his second year. However, as time passed, both Ms. Rekha and Sofi had left the college, leaving a void that was hard to fill.

Though they were no longer present in his daily life, their influence remained. Sai often thought about them—Rekha ma'am's unwavering belief in his potential and Sofi's warmth and laughter. He missed them both dearly, yet their absence also fueled his determination. He promised himself that he wouldn't allow these memories to distract him from his path. The girl he had met years ago during a competition, the one who unknowingly occupied his thoughts, was another story. He had tried countless times to forget her, telling himself there was no reason to hold on to someone he barely knew. But whenever he was sad, excited, or even the slightest bit lost, her face, though distant, would emerge from the depths of his mind.

Sai was now in his fifth semester, and though life had moved forward, there was still something unresolved. His goal was clear—he needed to keep his focus and continue excelling in his studies. Yet, fate seemed to have its own way of reminding him that certain bonds never truly fade. In his fifth semester, Sai was enrolled in a Communication Laboratory, a course designed to help students improve their language skills and professional communication. But what made this semester unusual was the teacher who would be handling the laboratory sessions—Ms. Madhu.

Ms. Madhu had been Sai's Technical English teacher during his first and second semesters. She was a young, charming woman with an infectious smile and a graceful demeanor. Back when she had first taught Sai, she was known for her strictness, maintaining a professional distance with her students. She wasn't harsh, but she set clear boundaries and expected nothing less than the best from her class. Sai remembered how, during his early days in college, he found Ms. Madhu's seriousness a bit intimidating. Yet, as the semesters passed, he began to notice something more in her—compassion hidden beneath her strict exterior.

When Sai found out that Ms. Madhu would be handling the same class again after a year, it came as a surprise. The college management typically rotated teachers, ensuring that no one instructor taught the same class twice in non-core subjects. However, this time, for reasons unknown, Ms. Madhu was back, and her approach was different—warmer, friendlier, and more familiar, like a mother reuniting with her children after a long separation.

Sai was initially puzzled by the change. Gone was the strict instructor from his first year. In her place stood someone who treated the class like her own family. She would joke with them, offer advice, and even listen to their personal struggles. Sai, in particular, noticed a special connection forming between him and Ms. Madhu.

During his first year, they had shared some conversations outside the classroom, moments where Sai had opened up about his personal goals, the pressure he felt from his department, and his struggles with some of the technical subjects. Ms. Madhu had been a patient listener, offering her own insights and words of encouragement. It wasn't long before she recognized that Sai was different from most students—quiet, thoughtful, and determined in his own way. Over time, she took it upon herself to keep an eye on him, guiding him through not just his English lessons but also through the challenges he faced in other areas.

In his third year, as academic pressures mounted, Sai found himself turning to Ms. Madhu for advice. Whenever he faced difficulties with his technical classes or felt overwhelmed by the demands of his department, Ms. Madhu was there, offering comfort and counsel. She wasn't just a teacher to him; she had become a mentor, someone who could sense when he was struggling even before he said a word.

Despite their growing bond, Sai always felt a sense of responsibility towards her. He admired her deeply for her motherly nature, the way she took care of every student in her class, ensuring they felt supported. He decided early on that he would make her proud by excelling in the

Communication Laboratory, just as he had done for Ms. Rekha in mathematics. His resolve was firm—he would get the best possible grade, not just for himself but for Ms. Madhu, as a way of thanking her for all her support.

However, the semester didn't unfold the way Sai had hoped. The Communication Laboratory was far more challenging than he had anticipated. While the content itself wasn't difficult, the pressure of the practical examinations, combined with the mounting workload from his other subjects, began to weigh on him. Despite his best efforts, he struggled to keep up.

The final blow came during the semester laboratory examination. The entire class was under immense stress, and technical glitches during the practicals made matters worse. Sai found himself making small but costly errors. The examiner was strict, and the mishaps during the lab led to a disastrous result—not just for Sai, but for the entire class.

When the grades were announced, Sai was devastated. He had aimed for a high score, but the final result was far below his expectations. Worse still, the entire class had received low grades, leading to widespread disappointment. For Sai, the pain wasn't just about the grade itself—it was about letting down Ms. Madhu.

Word of the results spread quickly, and soon, Ms. Madhu was informed. Sai knew she would be upset, but he wasn't prepared for how much it would affect her. When she came to the class after the results, there was a visible sadness in her eyes. The students had let her down, but more than that, she felt like she had failed them as a teacher.

Ms. Madhu stood at the front of the classroom, her usual warm demeanor replaced by a quiet resignation. She addressed the class, her voice filled with disappointment, but it wasn't harsh. It was the kind of disappointment a mother feels when her children don't live up to their potential.

"I believed in all of you," she said softly. "I thought we had built something strong together, that we were a team. But somewhere along the way, things fell apart."

Her words cut deep. Sai felt a lump in his throat as he listened. He had wanted to make her proud, but instead, he had contributed to this collective failure. Ms. Madhu's disappointment wasn't just with the class—it was with herself, and that was the hardest part for Sai to accept.

As she continued speaking, it became clear that this would be their last class together. Ms. Madhu announced that she would no longer be teaching their group after this semester. She didn't say it outright, but Sai knew that the poor results had played a part in her decision.

When the class ended, there was a heavy silence. Ms. Madhu gathered her things and left the room without looking back. Sai sat in his seat, unable to move. He had failed her, not just in the exam, but in the bond they had shared.

Over the next few days, Sai tried to come to terms with what had happened. He couldn't shake the feeling that he had let down someone who had believed in him, just like he had once feared disappointing Ms. Rekha. But this time, it felt different. This time, he had lost someone who had seen him not just as a student, but as a person.

In the end, the semester left Sai with a sense of loss. He had worked hard, built strong relationships, and tried to make those who cared about him proud. But life, as it often does, had thrown him an unexpected curve. He had learned that sometimes, despite your best efforts, things don't go as planned. And yet, amidst the disappointment,

Sai also found a renewed sense of purpose. He would take the lessons from this experience—both the successes and the failures—and carry them forward. Because that's what Ms. Madhu would have wanted.

10
A Week of Growth and New Beginning

—◆♡◆—

Sai started his next semester with newfound confidence. Despite the setbacks of the previous term, including the disappointment of the Communication Laboratory, he had resolved to push forward, armed with lessons from his past experiences. He understood now that success wasn't always linear, and the key was persistence. As the days rolled on, the air around campus began to buzz with excitement about an upcoming competition announced by one of the top universities in the country. The event was prestigious, known for gathering some of the brightest minds from across various fields of study.

For Sai, this competition represented more than just an opportunity to compete—it was a chance to prove to himself that he had what it took to shine beyond the confines of his own college. Many students from his institution were eager to participate, and when Sai learned that he had been selected to compete, he felt a surge of pride and excitement. Along with a few close friends, he would be representing his department, and together, they would head to the event with high expectations.

The university hosting the competition was renowned not only for its academic excellence but also for its sprawling, state-of-the-art campus. It was a place Sai had only heard about, and the idea of spending an entire week there—immersed in seminars, workshops, and challenges—was exhilarating. The event was designed to push the participants intellectually, socially, and creatively, making it a comprehensive experience unlike anything Sai had encountered before.

The day finally arrived, and Sai, along with a few other selected students, packed their bags and set off for the university. As their bus rolled into the campus gates, Sai was immediately struck by the sheer size and beauty of the place. Tall, modern buildings surrounded by lush greenery, wide walkways lined with trees, and the distant hum of students going about their day filled the atmosphere with a sense of purpose and energy. It felt like stepping into another world, a world where ideas thrived, and ambition was nurtured.

Upon their arrival, the participants were welcomed with a brief orientation session. The coordinators introduced the rules and guidelines that would be followed throughout the event. They explained that over the course of the week, students would engage in a mix of technical and creative sessions, and each team would be working on a unique problem statement assigned to them on the first day. Sai listened intently, eager to dive into the experience.

One of the most interesting aspects of the competition was the way the teams were formed. Rather than allowing students from the same college to stay together, the organizers had intentionally mixed everyone up. This meant that Sai and his friends would be placed in separate teams, alongside students from different institutions. At first, this made him a bit nervous—he had always felt most comfortable working with his close-knit group of friends—but he quickly realized the value of the experience. It was an opportunity to meet new people, learn from their perspectives, and grow beyond his comfort zone.

Sai's team consisted of students from various fields of study—some from engineering, others from business, the arts, and even medicine. There was a richness in the diversity of thought that immediately excited him. His teammates came from colleges spread across the country, each bringing their own unique set of skills and experiences to the table. Sai introduced himself and found that everyone was equally enthusiastic about the challenges ahead. They bonded quickly, their shared goal of excelling in the competition serving as a strong foundation for their teamwork.

The schedule for the week was packed. Each day would start early, with the mornings dedicated to seminars and workshops led by esteemed professors and industry experts. These sessions covered a wide range of topics, from cutting-edge technological advancements to discussions on global economic trends. Sai found himself soaking in the information like a sponge. Every speaker brought a different perspective, and the breadth of knowledge being shared was unlike anything he had experienced back at his own college.

But it wasn't just the technical aspects that made the event special. In the afternoons, the focus shifted to creative and life-skill training. Participants were encouraged to explore interests outside their academic fields, with sessions on cooking, singing, music, acting, and dance. Sai had never considered himself much of an artist, but he found these activities to be a refreshing change of pace. The cooking workshop, in particular, stood out to him—learning to make dishes from different cultures and working alongside his teammates to create something new brought a sense of joy and camaraderie that he hadn't expected.

Evenings were reserved for team collaboration. Each group had been assigned a unique problem statement on the first day, and they were tasked with developing a solution by the end of the week. The problem was complex and required a combination of technical knowledge, creativity, and strategic thinking. Sai's team worked late into the night, bouncing ideas off one another, testing theories, and refining their approach. He found himself growing more comfortable in this diverse group, appreciating the different perspectives that each member brought to the table. It was a true team effort, and the collaboration felt seamless.

Throughout the week, Sai also made time to explore the campus. The university was a vast and beautiful place, and whenever he had a few spare moments, he would wander through the gardens or sit by the serene lakes that dotted the grounds. The environment itself was inspiring, and Sai found that being in such a prestigious place only motivated him to push himself harder. He felt like he belonged here, among the best and brightest, and the sense of possibility was invigorating.

As the week progressed, Sai continued to meet new people—students from all corners of the country who had come to compete, learn, and grow. He built connections, exchanged ideas, and shared stories with his peers, finding that they all had one thing in common: a deep desire to make the most of this opportunity. The bonds he formed during this time weren't just with his teammates but with students from other colleges as well, many of whom he knew he would keep in touch with long after the competition ended.

The final day arrived all too soon. Each team presented their solutions to the panel of judges, who evaluated their work based on creativity, practicality, and presentation. Sai's team had worked tirelessly, and their final presentation was met with praise from the judges. Though they didn't win first place, Sai felt a deep sense of accomplishment. The experience had been far more valuable than any prize could offer. He had grown not just as a student, but as a person—developing communication skills, learning to work with others from different backgrounds, and gaining confidence in his own abilities.

As the event came to a close, Sai reflected on everything he had gained over the course of the week. He returned to his college with a sense of fulfillment and a bundle of new knowledge, friendships, and connections. The experience had broadened his horizons, both academically and socially. He had stepped out of his comfort zone, embraced new challenges, and discovered a new depth within himself.

On the bus ride back home, Sai felt a quiet sense of pride. He had faced the week with an open mind and heart, and in doing so, he had unlocked new possibilities for his future. The competition had not only expanded his academic understanding but also opened doors to new relationships and personal growth. He smiled to himself as the bus rolled down the highway, thinking of the friends he had made, the ideas he had explored, and the bright future that lay ahead.

11
The Changing Dynamics of Friendship

After the transformative week-long workshop at the top university, something had shifted inside Sai. The experience had opened him up to new perspectives, and he had begun to notice a change in the way he interacted with others, especially with his classmates. Prior to the event, Sai had always kept to himself or to his close circle of friends. He was reserved, hesitant to step beyond familiar boundaries, particularly when it came to interacting with girls. But now, something was different—he felt more at ease, more open to conversations and collaboration with others.

As Sai returned to his routine at college, he learned that his class would be merging with another section, effectively doubling the size of his peer group. This change gave him the opportunity to meet even more people, both boys and girls, from the other section. At first, the transition felt a bit overwhelming, with so many new faces to remember, but slowly, Sai began to embrace the chance to expand his friendships. The workshop had given him a newfound confidence, and he was now more willing to engage with his classmates—something he hadn't done much before. He began to participate more actively in group discussions, share his thoughts in class, and, for the first time, spend time with his female classmates without feeling awkward or out of place.

Sai's friend circle grew naturally, and with it, his understanding of people from different walks of life. One of the most significant changes he noticed was how he began to treat everyone the same, regardless of gender. He no longer felt the hesitation or discomfort that had once accompanied his interactions with girls. They were his peers, his friends, and he began to see them for who they were—individuals with unique personalities, thoughts, and ideas. This shift in perspective was liberating, and it allowed him to forge stronger connections within his class.

One day, while browsing through college announcements, Sai came across a seminar that seemed particularly interesting. Without giving it much thought, he posted about the event in a WhatsApp group that included many of the people he had met during the workshop. Little did he know that this simple act would lead to a new and meaningful friendship.

Among the people in the group was a girl named Mathi. She had been inspired by Sai's thoughts and ideas during the workshop, and his message about the seminar caught her attention. Despite living miles away, Mathi decided to travel all the way to Sai's college just to attend the event. She was eager to reconnect with him, having been impressed by his sincerity and thoughtfulness during their earlier interactions.

On the day of the seminar, Mathi texted Sai as soon as she reached the registration desk, unsure of where to go next. Sai called her immediately, guiding her step by step to the seminar hall. For Sai, this act of guiding and checking in on someone felt unfamiliar yet strangely natural. He found himself caring for her well-being, something he hadn't often experienced before, especially in such a casual, friendly way. As she approached the hall, Sai stood up and waved, his smile wide and welcoming.

Mathi greeted him with equal enthusiasm, and they took seats next to each other for the duration of the session. Throughout the seminar, Sai and Mathi exchanged thoughts, ideas, and jokes. Their conversation flowed easily, much like it had during the workshop, and Sai found himself enjoying her company more than he had anticipated. Mathi had a quick wit and a deep intellect, and her perspective often mirrored his own. They were, in many ways, kindred spirits. By the end of the seminar, they had become fast friends, and Mathi affectionately began calling him her "xerox copy," a nickname that reflected just how similar their thoughts and actions seemed to be.

Sai found comfort in this new friendship, appreciating how effortless it was to talk to Mathi. He felt no pretense, no need to prove anything. She understood him in a way that felt both familiar and refreshing. At the end of the session, they took a selfie together, capturing the moment of their newfound bond. Sai walked Mathi to the bus stand, making sure she boarded safely before heading back to his hostel. It had been a good day, one that left him feeling fulfilled and content.

Through Mathi, Sai was introduced to another new friend, Thara. Unlike his immediate connection with Mathi, Sai found it a bit harder to establish the same level of rapport with Thara. Although they interacted and had friendly conversations, there was always a subtle distance, a sense that they were acquaintances rather than close friends. Sai made an effort to connect with her, but something always seemed to keep them from becoming as close as he and Mathi had.

Months later, however, Thara reached out to Sai for technical support on a project she was working on. Sai, always ready to help a friend, stepped in and guided her through the problem. This interaction opened the door to more casual conversations, and while they didn't become as close as Sai and Mathi, there was now a sense of mutual respect and camaraderie between them. Sai had learned not to force friendships but to allow them to develop naturally.

For Sai, these experiences were eye-opening. He had spent much of his life keeping his distance from girls, partly out of a sense of discomfort and partly due to his own internalized beliefs about how relationships should work. But now, he found himself feeling differently. Spending time with Mathi, Thara, and other female classmates had taught him that relationships didn't have to be complicated. They could be simple, based on mutual respect, shared interests, and genuine friendship.

He realized that girls were not a mystery, nor were they something to be avoided or feared. They were people, just like him, with their own dreams, struggles, and quirks. And being in their company was enriching, offering him new insights and perspectives that he hadn't had before. The old Sai, who had avoided interaction with the opposite gender, seemed like a distant memory now. In their place stood a version of himself who was more open, understanding, and willing to embrace new experiences and friendships without hesitation.

As the semester progressed, Sai continued to grow and evolve. His time with Mathi and Thara, along with his other classmates, had taught him the importance of balance in relationships. He no longer saw gender as a barrier or something that separated him from others. Instead, he viewed everyone through the same lens of friendship and mutual respect. The more he opened up, the more he realized how much he had been missing by keeping to himself all those years.

In conclusion, Sai found that the company of girls was not only valuable but necessary. They had helped him grow in ways he hadn't expected, pushing him to understand himself better and to break free from the limitations he had placed on his own social interactions. He now saw friendships for what they were—beautiful connections that transcended gender and were built on trust, understanding, and shared experiences.

12

The Familiar Face and Fading Connection

One ordinary afternoon, Sai was walking down the pathway near his college cafeteria. He had gone out for lunch, his mind preoccupied with the usual hustle and bustle of college life—assignments, exams, and the never-ending whirlwind of activities. But as he strolled along, something caught his eye—a girl walking ahead of him. She seemed familiar, triggering a distant memory he couldn't quite place. He slowed his pace, squinting in an attempt to remember where he had seen her before.

As the girl passed by, Sai's thoughts whirred. He knew he had seen her somewhere, but the memory felt blurry, like a picture out of focus. The girl didn't seem to recognize him, walking confidently, her mind elsewhere. Her presence lingered with Sai even after she was gone from sight. He spent the next few minutes trying to connect the dots, until a sudden realization hit him—she had studied in his school. But there was more. She wasn't just any student; she had been part of the biology group, while Sai had been in the computer science group. He had seen her in school on a few occasions, mostly in passing, but they had never interacted.

Sai's curiosity deepened. He felt an inexplicable urge to reconnect with her, to see if she remembered their shared history in school. After all, they had once walked the same corridors, shared the same schoolyard, and yet, they had never exchanged more than a glance.

He started by reaching out to one of his old school friends, who was now studying BDS at another college. This friend, a trusted confidante from Sai's school days, would surely remember her. After a brief chat, his friend confirmed that the girl's name was Aditi, and she indeed had studied in Sai's school. The pieces of the puzzle were falling into place, but now the question was—how could Sai reach out to her?

Sai's friend casually mentioned that Aditi was active on WhatsApp and social media, leaving Sai with the idea of messaging her. He hesitated for a moment, unsure of how to initiate a conversation with someone who likely didn't even remember him. But his curiosity got the better of him, and before long, he had tracked down her number through a mutual contact.

Sai's heart raced as he typed his first message. He kept it simple, hoping to jog her memory without seeming too forward: "Hi Aditi, do you remember me? We were in the same school, though in different groups. I'm Sai, from the computer science group." He hit send and waited, his thoughts bouncing between excitement and nervousness.

Hours passed with no reply. Sai figured she might not remember him, or worse, wasn't interested in talking. The next day, however, his phone buzzed with a notification. Aditi had replied: "Who is this? Do I know you?" Her tone felt distant, as if she had no recollection of him at all.

Sai tried to explain, reminding her of their time in school and the few times he had seen her. But the conversation didn't flow the way he had hoped. After a few short, clipped responses, Aditi blocked him on WhatsApp. The abruptness of it stung, but Sai shrugged it off, telling himself that it wasn't worth dwelling on. He had tried, and that was enough.

Life went on as usual. Sai buried himself in his studies, his projects, and his college routine. Aditi was a fleeting thought, something that had passed as quickly as it had come. Yet, fate had other plans.

Weeks later, on a random day, Sai was forwarding some memes and funny videos to his contacts list. It was something he did without much thought, a way to pass the time. Unbeknownst to him, one of those forwards ended up being sent to Aditi, who was still saved in his contacts.

Aditi's reply was almost instantaneous: "Who is this?" Sai stared at the message, surprised. Had she forgotten their previous conversation? He reminded her of their brief exchange weeks ago, the one where she had blocked him. To his relief, this time Aditi seemed more open to conversation. She apologized for blocking him, admitting she had been overwhelmed at the time. With that, the door to communication was reopened.

Over the next few days, Sai and Aditi began talking more frequently. The awkwardness of their initial exchanges slowly melted away as they found common ground. They discovered that they shared a similar sense of humor and a few overlapping interests, and their conversations became more fluid, more natural. Aditi, Sai found out, was studying BDS on the same campus but in a different department, which explained why they had never crossed paths before.

As their friendship grew, they began spending more time together. They would sometimes run into each other on campus, and occasionally, they would sit together during lunch breaks, chatting about their college lives and the memories of their hometown. Their conversations were effortless, and they began to feel a sense of comfort in each other's company.

Rumors, of course, started to spread. People began to notice how often Sai and Aditi were together, and whispers circulated that they might be more than friends. It was inevitable, given the nature of college life, but neither Sai nor Aditi paid much attention to the gossip. They knew what their bond was—close, but not romantic.

One day, as they were walking together, the topic came up. Aditi turned to Sai and asked, half-jokingly, "Do people really think we're in love?" Sai chuckled, shrugging it off. "Seems like it," he replied. "But we know the truth."

They sat down on a bench, the afternoon sun casting long shadows around them. "I like being with you," Sai admitted. "You're good company, and it's nice to have someone to talk to about everything."

Aditi nodded, her smile gentle but firm. "Same here. But we both know it's not love, right? We're just... good friends."

Sai agreed, relieved that they were on the same page. They shared a laugh, the tension dissolving. They concluded that while they enjoyed each other's company, they weren't in love. It was a friendship based on mutual respect and understanding, not romantic feelings.

But as their conversations became less frequent and their meetups more sporadic, Sai began to notice a subtle shift. Life moved on, and slowly, their friendship faded into the background. Eventually, their daily chats turned into weekly check-ins, and soon, they stopped talking altogether.

It wasn't a conscious decision, but the natural course of things. They had grown close, shared experiences, and eventually drifted apart.

During this time, as Sai reflected on his connection with Aditi, his mind wandered to another girl—one he hadn't thought about in a long time. A girl he had seen at a competition years ago, who had left a lasting impression on him, even though he had never spoken to her. This thought began to surface more frequently, especially as his conversations with Aditi dwindled. The girl from the competition had been a fleeting presence in his life, but for some reason, her memory clung to him like a shadow.

Sai found himself thinking about her more and more, wondering why she had made such an impact on him. Was it the mystery of her presence, the fact that he had never had the chance to speak to her? Or was it something deeper, something unspoken? He couldn't quite pin it down, but the memory of her lingered in his mind, like a puzzle waiting to be solved.

As Sai continued with his college life, he tried to push the thoughts away, but they kept coming back, especially in quiet moments. He realized that, for some reason, this girl had left a mark on him, one that wouldn't easily fade.

13
The Symposium Spark

In Sai's department, an unexpected decision was made that year—to give the responsibility of organizing the annual Technical Symposium to the third-year students instead of the final year. This change came as a surprise, but it excited Sai and his peers. It was a rare opportunity to lead such a significant event, and Sai decided to take ownership of several key activities. This symposium would not only be a platform for showcasing technical knowledge but also a chance to build relationships with juniors and seniors.

Sai quickly immersed himself in the preparations, collaborating with students from different years. There was a lot of energy and excitement in the air as they brainstormed event ideas, prepared technical papers, and organized workshops. He worked closely with senior boys and girls, some of whom he had rarely interacted with before. They spent long hours discussing the event, and in that time, Sai got to know them on a deeper level. Conversations flowed easily—about academics, life, and the future. There was a shared sense of purpose and collaboration among them all, as everyone wanted the symposium to be a success.

While working with his peers, Sai began to see himself from a new perspective. He discovered that others saw him as a leader, someone who could take charge and inspire. Many admired him for his dedication, knowledge, and calm demeanor. Through casual conversations with juniors and seniors, he learned how his actions were quietly influencing others. His behavior and intelligence had made an impression on many, something he hadn't realized before.

Preparations continued late into the night in the days leading up to the event. The campus buzzed with activity—teams were busy arranging the venue, setting up banners, and organizing the flow of the symposium. Sai was everywhere, overseeing tasks, ensuring everything was on track. He bonded with his peers over endless cups of coffee in the cafeteria, chatting about the challenges ahead and their excitement for the event. They shared jokes, frustrations, and ideas, building a strong camaraderie.

During one of these casual moments in the cafeteria, the conversation turned to Aditi. A few senior girls, curious about Sai's connection with her, decided to call her. They asked for her opinion about him, teasing Sai with playful remarks. This moment, though light-hearted, stirred something within him—a strange feeling of disconnect. Perhaps this was the beginning of the fading bond with Aditi, though he didn't dwell on it too much at the time. Sai was focused on the present, on making the symposium a success.

The night before the event was a whirlwind. The entire team worked through the night, finalizing decorations, checking equipment, and ensuring every detail was perfect. The campus, usually quiet at that hour, was alive with the hum of excitement. The event day finally arrived, and with it came a sense of exhaustion but also exhilaration. Sai had barely slept, but adrenaline kept him going.

As the symposium kicked off, Sai found himself sitting in a hall, overseeing a technical paper presentation. He had become the go-to person for managing the presentations, handling questions, and ensuring everything ran smoothly. The room was packed with students, faculty, and guests from other colleges, all eager to witness the showcase of technical skills.

In the midst of the presentations, a group of girls from other college struggled with their paper. They were unable to answer the tough technical questions posed by the judges, visibly anxious and flustered. Seeing their distress, Sai couldn't sit back and watch. Without hesitation, he stepped in on their behalf, answering some of the questions with confidence and helping them regain their composure. His intervention not only saved the moment but also impressed everyone in the room.

During the event, Sai also met a few people outside of his college, including some seniors from other institutions. Although these interactions were brief, they left an impression on him. It was clear that his network was expanding beyond the confines of his own campus, and these new connections would likely prove valuable in the future.

As the symposium drew to a close, Sai was physically and mentally exhausted. He had given everything to ensure its success, and the satisfaction of seeing it all come together was worth every sleepless night. Sitting alone in the empty presentation hall after the event, he allowed himself a moment of reflection. He had learned so much—not just about organizing events but also about himself, about leadership, and about how others viewed him.

That evening, he joined his team for one last celebratory meal. They laughed, reminisced about the week leading up to the event, and shared stories about the funny moments and near disasters they had overcome. There was a sense of accomplishment in the air—a feeling that they had done something truly remarkable together.

Sai's thoughts drifted back to the senior girls he had gotten to know during the symposium, especially the ones who had playfully called Aditi. Though that connection was fading, he realized that the relationships he was building with his classmates and seniors were more important now. These were the people he would lean on in the coming years, and they would be the ones to shape his college experience going forward.

As he walked back to his room that night, utterly spent, Sai felt a quiet sense of pride. The symposium had been a test of his capabilities, and he had passed. More than that, it had shown him the importance of working together, of building connections, and of leading with kindness and confidence. He had grown, not just as a student, but as a person.

14
Bond Beyond Boundaries

The symposium had come to an end, but the events of the previous day still lingered in Sai's mind. He had stepped in during a technical presentation and helped a group of girls from another college who were struggling with their answers. It wasn't just that they needed assistance—it was that their topic piqued his interest in ways he hadn't anticipated. The group had been presenting on a concept related to Electromagnetic Fields (EMF), a subject Sai was particularly strong in. However, what intrigued him the most was the innovative application they were proposing. It was something new, something beyond what he had explored.

The next morning, Sai woke up to a quiet weekend. His thoughts were still on that project. He made his way to a nearby café, seeking the calm atmosphere and the aroma of freshly brewed coffee. Laptop in hand, he settled into a cozy corner, eager to dive into the technical writeups the symposium team had received. Logging into the event's organizing email account, he began sifting through the technical papers submitted for publication. He had been tasked with reviewing them for journal submission, a responsibility he took seriously.

As he read through the various papers, he stumbled upon the one written by the group of girls he had helped. Their work focused on applying EMF principles to a new kind of sensor technology, something Sai found incredibly fascinating. As he read their writeup, his curiosity grew. He wanted to learn more, not just theoretically, but practically—how could this concept be brought to life as a working prototype?

He decided to reach out. From the symposium registration forms, he found the group's email addresses. Without hesitation, he composed a message from his personal account, introducing himself and expressing his interest in their work. He was straightforward but polite, sharing his passion for EMF and explaining how he had been captivated by their application of the concept. He offered to collaborate, stating his willingness to contribute his expertise in exchange for the opportunity to learn more about their project and the potential hardware implementation.

Hours later, his inbox chimed with a reply. One of the girls, Vidhu, responded. She was the heart of their group, the one who had taken the lead during the presentation. In her email, she was warm and welcoming, appreciating Sai's offer to collaborate. Over the next few days, their conversations deepened as they exchanged ideas, technical documents, and designs. What started as a purely academic exchange soon blossomed into a friendship. Sai found himself drawn to Vidhu's intelligence and her ability to explain complex ideas with ease. She, in turn, admired his dedication and the depth of his knowledge in EMF.

As they continued to work on the project, Vidhu and Sai grew closer—not just as collaborators, but as friends. Despite being from different colleges and different walks of life, their bond strengthened. Vidhu, being slightly older, took on the role of an elder sister in Sai's life. She saw potential in him, not just in his technical abilities but in his character. She began guiding him in ways that extended beyond academics.

Vidhu noticed how Sai interacted with others, especially girls, and she saw room for growth. She started to teach him about manners—how to be more considerate, how to engage in meaningful conversations, and how to handle situations with grace. She often teased him, calling him her "little brother," but there was always a warmth behind her words. Sai found her guidance invaluable. He had never had a sister before, but with Vidhu, he felt like he had gained one. She filled a gap in his life that he hadn't even realized existed.

Their bond extended beyond the project. They would chat late into the night, not just about technical work but about life, dreams, and the future. Vidhu shared her aspirations, her struggles, and her journey through college, while Sai opened up about his own experiences and ambitions. She became his confidant, someone he could trust implicitly. Their conversations often drifted from electromagnetism to the subtle nuances of human behavior, and Vidhu's advice became a cornerstone of Sai's growth.

One evening, while they were discussing the progress of their project, Vidhu gently broached a subject that had been on her mind. "Sai," she said, "you're brilliant, but sometimes I feel like you don't know how to fully express yourself around others, especially girls. You're respectful, yes, but there's more to it. It's about understanding emotions, reading people's feelings."

Sai listened intently. He hadn't given much thought to the way he interacted with others, particularly with girls. He had always been focused on his studies, on his technical skills, but Vidhu's words made him reflect on how important emotional intelligence was. Over the next few weeks, under Vidhu's mentorship, Sai became more self-aware. He learned how to navigate social interactions with greater ease, how to communicate with empathy, and how to listen more deeply.

Their project neared completion, and they began working on the prototype. The long hours of coding, designing, and troubleshooting became a shared journey. Whenever they hit a roadblock, Vidhu would encourage Sai to keep going, reminding him that persistence was key to success. And whenever Sai had a breakthrough, Vidhu was the first to celebrate with him.

Finally, the day arrived when the prototype was complete. Sai and Vidhu, along with the rest of their team, presented their work to a panel of judges. The feedback was overwhelmingly positive, and they were commended for their innovative approach. For Sai, this project wasn't just a technical achievement—it was a turning point in his personal growth.

At the end of the symposium, as everyone was packing up, Vidhu gave Sai a tight hug. "You did great, little brother," she said, smiling warmly. "I'm proud of you, not just for the project, but for how much you've grown."

Sai smiled back, feeling a deep sense of gratitude. "I couldn't have done it without you, Vidhu," he replied. "You've taught me so much—more than you know."

As they parted ways, Sai realized that Vidhu had become more than just a mentor or a teammate. She was family, a sister he would always cherish. Though the project was over, their bond would remain. And in the process, Sai had not only completed a challenging technical project but had also gained invaluable lessons about life, relationships, and the importance of emotional intelligence.

15
The Turning Point

With every new experience, Sai felt like he was evolving. The week-long workshop had been a catalyst for change, and the symposium had only deepened his understanding of teamwork, communication, and collaboration. He had learned so much from people he hadn't known a few weeks before, and he was filled with a new energy. It wasn't just about the academic or technical growth—he was beginning to understand the value of building connections, of learning from others, and of finding a balance between hard work and relationships.

As the semester exams approached, Sai knew that the stakes were high. This semester, two subjects loomed large in his mind: Computer Networks and VLSI. Both seemed like insurmountable challenges at first. He had struggled to grasp the complexities of network layers, protocols, and the intricacies of integrated circuit design. The textbooks felt dense, and each chapter seemed to introduce a new set of concepts that built on the last.

Sai was determined, though. The newfound confidence he had developed during the symposium drove him forward. He knew that if he could work hard enough, if he could apply the same principles of focus and dedication that he had used during the project work, he could conquer these subjects too. He started from the basics, treating each concept as though he were learning it for the first time. He watched online tutorials, scoured through textbooks, and spent hours in the library. His study schedule became intense.

His friends noticed the shift in him. Vidhu, in particular, had become a pillar of support. She had helped him navigate so many challenges over the past few months, and now she was there for him again. Though they were from different colleges, their bond remained strong. Sai often called her after his long study sessions, sharing his doubts or frustrations. Vidhu, who was equally committed to her own studies, would patiently listen and then explain concepts in a way that made them easier to understand.

One evening, as Sai sat in the college cafeteria with his laptop and a pile of notes, he found himself struggling with a particularly challenging topic in Computer Networks: subnetting. No matter how many times he read the material, it seemed impossible to grasp. The clock on the wall ticked past midnight, and the cafeteria, once bustling with students, was now almost empty. The exhaustion was starting to wear him down, but he knew he couldn't afford to stop. He reached out to Vidhu.

"Hey, I'm stuck," he typed into his phone.

It didn't take long for her to reply. "What's up?"

He explained his confusion, and within minutes, they were on a call. Vidhu guided him through the steps, breaking down the problem into manageable pieces, and suddenly, it all clicked. It wasn't just about understanding the material anymore—it was about having someone who believed in him, someone who could help him see things from a different perspective.

It wasn't only Vidhu who supported him. His classmates, particularly the girls who were excelling academically, became a crucial part of his study group. They had already scored well in the internal exams, and they were more than willing to help Sai with his preparation. These sessions often turned into long nights, sitting together in the library or grabbing a quick meal in the canteen, pouring over notes and past papers. They worked through complex problems, shared study techniques, and encouraged each other.

Control Systems was another subject that Sai had struggled with in the past. The dreaded Bode and Pole plots had once seemed like an unsolvable mystery, an impenetrable wall that stood between him and passing the subject. But this time, with the help of his friends, he approached it with a new perspective. One of his classmates, who had always aced the subject, sat with him for hours, explaining the finer details of the plots, showing him how to break them down, how to read and analyze them. Sai was relentless in his practice. He drew graph after graph, plotted pole after pole, until it became second nature.

Late nights became a routine. Sai would often find himself awake at 3 a.m., still deep into his books, his mind whirring with information, trying to absorb everything before the exams. The fatigue was real, but so was his determination. Some nights, when he couldn't bear to be alone with his thoughts, he would text his friends, and they'd meet up in the cafeteria or the campus garden. Together, they would sip on hot tea or coffee, their conversations alternating between lighthearted jokes and intense study sessions.

Sai's days started blending into nights. He would wake up, attend his classes, and immediately dive into his preparation. Even meals became secondary. He often skipped breakfast, grabbing something quick in between study sessions. Lunch was a hurried affair, with his notes spread out in front of him at the table. Dinner, when he remembered to have it, was usually eaten late, after the library closed.

But despite the exhaustion, there was a fire in him. He wanted to not only pass but excel. The internal exams had gone well, giving him a boost of confidence. His lab work, particularly in VLSI, became another area where he poured in extra hours. He spent long afternoons in the laboratory, working through the practicals, making sure he understood every step, every calculation.

His final lab exams were challenging but manageable, and Sai walked out of each one feeling more accomplished. Control Systems, the subject that had once haunted him, was now something he could handle with ease, thanks to the hours of preparation and the guidance of his friends.

As the exams neared their conclusion, Sai began thinking about the future. The semester break was approaching, and he didn't want to waste it. For him, holidays had never been about relaxation—they were an opportunity to learn, to grow, and to explore new ideas. He made a decision: this break, he would do something meaningful. Whether it was taking up a new course, working on a project, or diving into a topic he had always wanted to explore, he was determined not to let this time slip by idly.

The sleepless nights, the study sessions with friends, the moments of frustration and triumph—all of it was leading him toward something greater. Sai could feel it. The semester had been tough, but it had also been transformative. He had learned not just about Computer Networks or Control Systems but about himself, about perseverance, about the value of friendship and collaboration.

And as he packed up his books and walked out of the cafeteria that night, he knew that the next part of his journey was just beginning.

With all the hard work, sleepless nights, and intense study sessions behind him, Sai finally walked into the examination hall for the final set of exams. As he sat there, pencil in hand, flipping through the question paper, he felt a calmness he hadn't expected. Every question that had once seemed impossible now felt manageable. The hours of preparation paid off. Whether it was the complex subnetting problems in Computer Networks or the intricacies of VLSI circuits, Sai tackled each question with confidence.

He could feel the difference. His mind was sharper, his thoughts clearer. The Bode and Pole plots, which had once felt like an unsolvable puzzle, were now something he could visualize in his head. As he scribbled his answers and solved the calculations, there was no longer any panic—just focus. The practical lab exams went smoothly as well. Sai moved through the experiments with ease, ensuring each step was precise and calculated. When he finally handed in his last answer sheet and walked out of the exam hall, there was a sense of accomplishment washing over him.

He had done it. He had faced the challenge head-on, and now, it was over. The semester that had tested him in every way was finally behind him, and he couldn't help but smile.

As Sai packed up his books and materials, the exhaustion from the previous weeks began to fade, replaced by a deep sense of relief. He had performed well—better than he could have imagined—and now he had a break ahead of him, free from the stress of exams. But even though the semester had ended, Sai didn't see the holidays as a time for relaxation. He had already made plans to spend his time wisely.

As he walked out of the college gates that evening, the cool evening breeze felt like freedom. His mind buzzed with possibilities. Sai had always been someone who thrived on learning, and now, with weeks ahead of him free from academic pressure, he was ready to dive into new opportunities.

His phone buzzed with messages from his classmates and friends, all expressing their relief at the exams being over. Some talked about travel plans, others about catching up on sleep, but for Sai, the semester break was a chance to explore something different.

The conversation with Vidhu and his other friends had left him with a lot to think about. They had all played such an important role in helping him get through the exams, and he couldn't help but reflect on how much he had grown, not just academically, but also as a person. Sai realized that it wasn't just the subjects he had mastered—it was his ability to push through challenges, to ask for help when needed, and to give back to those who supported him.

He spent the first few days of the break unwinding, spending time with his friends and family, catching up on the little moments he had missed during his intense study sessions. But even during these moments of rest, his mind was constantly thinking about what he would do next. There were so many things he wanted to learn, projects he wanted to work on, and ideas he wanted to explore.

Sai's determination to make the most of his holidays wasn't just about gaining more knowledge; it was about building on the momentum he had created during the semester. He didn't want to lose the rhythm he had found in the last few months, and he knew that if he continued to work hard, the next semester would be even better.

As he sat at his desk, looking out the window at the setting sun, Sai smiled to himself. The exams were behind him, but the journey was far from over. With the same energy and enthusiasm that had driven him through the semester, he was ready to take on whatever came next. The break was just the beginning of a new chapter—one that promised growth, learning, and a future full of possibilities.

16

New Horizons

The semester exams had finally wrapped up, and with a sense of accomplishment, he embraced the freedom that came with the holiday. This break was not just a time to relax; he was determined to make the most of it. The pressure of the upcoming placements loomed over him, but he felt a glimmer of hope when he heard about an internship opportunity at a prestigious MNC. It was the chance he had been waiting for—a way to gain valuable experience and make connections in the industry.

After applying, he received the exciting news that he was accepted for the internship. Over the next month, he immersed himself in the corporate environment, learning the ropes and networking with professionals who had once seemed so distant. The contacts he made were invaluable, opening doors to insights about the industry and potential job opportunities after graduation. Each day was a new learning experience, and he relished the challenges that came with the role.

During his time at the MNC, he couldn't help but notice a couple who worked closely together. They shared laughter and exchanged knowing glances, their chemistry palpable in the office. Each time he saw them, a pang of nostalgia struck him, reminding him of the girl he had met a year ago during a college competition. The memory of their brief encounter lingered in his mind, a bittersweet reminder of what could have been.

As he observed their relationship, something within him shifted. His perspective on love and connection began to change. He realized that he had been holding onto an idealized version of the girl he had met, but now he started to accept her presence in his life. Thoughts of her transformed from mere memories into a motivation to seek her out again. He felt a renewed determination to express his feelings for her, to not let the opportunity slip away again.

As the internship came to an end, he returned to college, bringing back not only newfound knowledge but also a renewed determination. The semester was just beginning, and the pressure of placements was palpable. His peers buzzed with excitement and anxiety, each one eager to secure a job that would pave the way for their future.

He dived into placement preparations with a fervor he had never experienced before. Long nights were spent reviewing resumes, practicing interview questions, and attending workshops that the college organized to prepare students for the competitive world outside. The thought of the upcoming on-campus placement drive loomed over him, intensifying his focus. The company that had invited them was known for selecting candidates from various colleges, and he wanted to stand out among them.

As the date approached, he felt a mix of nerves and excitement. This was it—a chance to showcase everything he had learned, both in college and during his internship. He spent every free moment revising and rehearsing, determined to make a strong impression. The night before the placement drive, he could barely sleep, his mind racing with thoughts of the interviews and the opportunity that awaited him.

On the day of the placement drive, the campus was abuzz with energy. Students from different colleges mingled, exchanging pleasantries and anxieties. As he entered the interview hall, he took a deep breath, grounding himself in the moment. This was his chance to make a lasting impression, and he was ready to seize it.

17
The Interview Day

———♡———

The day of the interview had finally arrived, filling the campus with a palpable buzz of anticipation. Students hustled through the corridors, their faces a mixture of excitement and anxiety. He felt a familiar blend of both emotions as he prepared to enter the auditorium for the placement session. Having returned to college a month late, he was determined not to miss this vital opportunity. Still, a sense of hesitation lingered. Would he be at a disadvantage for arriving late?

As he approached the classroom, he caught a glimpse of her—the girl from the college competition. She was stepping up the staircase, her presence captivating. With each step, her long hair cascaded over her shoulders, catching the light and shining like silk. She wore a simple yet elegant outfit that complemented her figure, enhancing her natural beauty. He couldn't help but notice the way her eyes sparkled with enthusiasm as she chatted with her friends, laughter spilling effortlessly from her lips.

For a moment, he was lost in admiration, the world around him fading as he took in her radiance. Memories of their brief encounter flooded back, stirring feelings he had kept at bay. With determination surging through him, he refocused on the interview. He had to make the most of this chance, despite the flutter of nerves twisting in his stomach.

He made his way toward the auditorium, where the placement interviews would take place. As he entered, the atmosphere buzzed with chatter and anticipation. He scanned the rows and spotted her sitting in the third row, engaged in conversation with a couple of classmates. She was as captivating as he remembered, her laughter ringing in the air like music, making his heart race.

But as he moved closer, a wave of apprehension washed over him. He hadn't registered for the interview; the realization hit him like a cold splash of water. Would he really be able to go through with this? Taking a deep breath, he approached the placement coordinator.

"Excuse me," he said, trying to keep his voice steady. "I know it's late, but is there any way I can attend the interviews today?"

The coordinator looked him over, then sighed. "We can make that happen, but you'll need to help me out. You'll have to collect the answer sheets from all the candidates after the interviews and hand them back to me, along with their resumes."

His heart raced at the prospect. This was not only a chance to participate in the interviews but also an opportunity to gather information about her. "Absolutely," he replied eagerly, the determination in his voice unmistakable.

As he took his seat in the last row of the auditorium, he felt a surge of hope. He could see her clearly from his position, and the sight ignited a spark of excitement in him. The process began, and while he listened to the interviews unfold, his thoughts wandered to the details he could collect. Perhaps he could find her resume, at least get her name or contact information.

The interviews lasted for about an hour. He sat there, 20 or 25 seats away, trying to catch glimpses of her through the narrow space between rows. Each time he saw her smile or heard her voice, he felt a sense of happiness wash over him, mingled with the frustration of being unable to reach out to her.

Finally, as the session drew to a close, he quickly gathered his courage and approached his friends. "Hey, can you help me collect the papers?" he asked, desperation creeping into his voice. They agreed, and with their assistance, he managed to gather most of the answer sheets and resumes.

But just as he was about to leave, he realized her paper had slipped into the hands of another friend. Panic surged through him. He had to find her resume, to learn about the girl who had unknowingly captivated his heart all those months ago.

He found a hidden spot inside the auditorium and began to sift through the collected papers. With each sheet he flipped, hope surged within him, but as he searched for one specific resume, he felt the familiar ache of disappointment creeping in. The moment he was hoping for seemed just out of reach.

As he continued to sift through the pile of answer sheets and resumes, a sense of urgency settled in. Each paper he examined felt like a fleeting moment slipping through his fingers, each one potentially holding her name, her story. He carefully scrutinized every detail, searching for that familiar spark of connection that had ignited in him the day they first met.

But as he moved through the papers, his heart sank further. The familiar faces and names of his classmates filled the sheets, but none were hers. With each resume he flipped through, he felt the weight of disappointment settling on his shoulders. She could be just a name, an unfamiliar face in a sea of papers, and yet, the desire to know her felt like an urgent flame within him.

Finally, as he reached the last few sheets, he noticed a different font. He held his breath, praying for that familiar rush of recognition. But the name he found was not hers; it belonged to another girl entirely. Frustration boiled within him, and he slammed the paper down, the sound echoing in the quiet corner where he sat.

"What's wrong?" his friend asked, peering over his shoulder.

"I'm just trying to find someone I saw earlier," he admitted, disappointment lacing his voice. "But I can't find her resume anywhere."

His friend shrugged sympathetically. "Maybe she didn't register for the placement? Sometimes students miss these opportunities."

Those words felt like a punch to the gut. What if she hadn't registered? What if fate had conspired against him once again, pulling her just out of reach? The fleeting moments they had shared hung in the air, both bittersweet and tantalizing, as he contemplated the chances he had missed.

The realization settled like a heavy blanket over him. He had seen her, but he might never know her name or contact information. His determination to find her, to reconnect and express the feelings he had nurtured in silence, felt impossibly far away.

Sighing, he gathered the remaining sheets and stood up, making his way back to the front of the auditorium. As he approached the placement coordinator, a familiar voice echoed in the background, bringing him to a halt.

"Thank you all for your participation today! We will be in touch with the results very soon!"

He turned slowly, heart racing. There she was, standing among a cluster of students, her laughter light and joyful. The way she interacted with her friends only amplified the ache in his chest. He wanted to join her, to step out of the shadows and into her light, but fear held him back.

As the crowd began to disperse, he felt a strange mix of hope and despair. The opportunity to reconnect seemed to be slipping away, and the thought of losing her again sent a chill down his spine. Determined not to let this chance slip away, he took a deep breath and walked toward her.

But as he approached, she was swept away by her friends, their voices rising above the din of the departing crowd. He felt a pang of longing as he watched her go, her image fading into the throng of students.

Despite the disappointment that weighed heavily on him, he knew one thing for certain: he couldn't give up. This wasn't the end of his search. As he stepped outside, the sun bathed the campus in warm light, a stark contrast to the turmoil in his heart. He would find a way to connect with her again. This time, he would make sure it counted.

The journey ahead was uncertain, but one thing was clear—he would not let fear dictate his next steps. With determination burning bright within him, he resolved to seek her out, to uncover the name that had eluded him, and to finally express the feelings that had taken root in his heart.

18

A Journey of Connection

As the weeks rolled by, Sai found himself increasingly engrossed in his studies. Yet, amid the constant swirl of equations and theories, thoughts of her—the girl from the college competition—intertwined with his academic life like a melody that wouldn't fade away. Each time he opened his textbook or scribbled notes, fragments of their brief encounter danced in his mind, urging him to connect again, to find a way to turn those fleeting moments into something lasting.

In the midst of his academic pursuits, Sai was also determined to improve Vidhu's project. It had the potential to stand out, and he wanted to take it to the next level. He spent countless hours brainstorming ideas, poring over research articles, and discussing possibilities with his friend. With each passing day, he felt a sense of purpose wash over him; he wasn't just working for grades anymore—he was working for something meaningful.

But academic life had its own demands. As the deadline for the project submission approached, he realized he needed to present their work for publication in a journal. It was a significant step, and the thought of contributing something valuable made his heart race with excitement. Sai began searching for colleges around their region that might host events focused on academic publishing, eager to find the perfect opportunity to showcase their project.

After a few days of diligent research, a notification popped up on his screen: an upcoming event at her college, featuring opportunities for students to present their work. The moment he saw it, his heart skipped a beat. This could be his chance—not just to present their project but also to see her again. He could hardly believe his luck; fate seemed to be throwing him a lifeline, and he was determined to grasp it with both hands.

The following day, with a mix of nerves and excitement, Sai revealed his feelings to Vidhu. "I think I'm in love with her," he confessed, the words tumbling out before he could think twice.

Vidhu's eyes widened in shock, a surprised smile creeping onto his face. "Wait, what? You're serious?" he asked, unable to hide his astonishment.

"Yeah," Sai said, his cheeks flushing slightly. "I mean, I've been thinking about her a lot. I just want to see her again, to talk to her."

Vidhu's expression shifted from shock to happiness. "That's amazing! I'm really happy for you, man. You should go for it. This is your chance!"

Sai felt a wave of relief wash over him. It was one thing to have feelings for someone, but sharing them with his friend made it feel more real. With Vidhu's encouragement, he set his sights on the upcoming event with renewed determination.

On the day of the presentation, Sai arrived at her college, nerves dancing in his stomach like butterflies. He was excited yet anxious, his mind racing with possibilities of what could unfold. After presenting their project to a panel of professors, he felt a sense of accomplishment, but it quickly faded into a familiar yearning. He needed to find her.

As his friends left, content with the day's achievements, Sai decided to stay behind. He wandered the campus, his heart pounding with every corner he turned, hoping to catch a glimpse of her. The familiar buildings, bustling students, and vibrant atmosphere were both comforting and overwhelming.

Just when he thought he might leave without seeing her, he spotted her in the distance. She wore a smart blazer, her hair falling gracefully over her shoulders as she chatted with friends. She was radiant, carrying a file filled with documents, and there was a lightness in her demeanor that made his heart soar. It was as if she radiated happiness.

Gathering his courage, Sai took a step forward, intending to say hi, but she seemed lost in conversation and didn't notice him. Disappointment flickered through him, but he refused to let it deter him. Instead, he followed her to the cafeteria, where she sat alone at a table, blissfully unaware of his presence.

From a distance, he watched her enjoy her lunch, the way she smiled at her friends and laughed at their jokes. In that moment, it struck him how beautiful she looked, completely in her element. He felt a wave of nostalgia wash over him, recalling the fleeting connection they had shared during the college competition.

As he sat there, hidden in a corner, he felt a mix of emotions—happiness to see her, sadness for not being able to speak with her, and a longing that felt unquenchable. He wished he could share his feelings, express the depth of what he had experienced since that day. But for now, he was content to simply watch her, to relish the sight of someone who had unwittingly captured his heart.

Eventually, after what felt like an eternity, he decided it was time to leave. He didn't want to overstay his welcome or come off as too eager. With one last lingering glance at her, he turned to head back to his college, a smile spreading across his face despite the bittersweet ache in his heart. The day had brought him joy, even if it hadn't ended as he had hoped.

Back in his own college, he dove headfirst into exam preparations and the final touches of their project submission. With the end of the semester drawing near, the intensity of his studies surged. He felt focused and determined, fueled not just by the desire to succeed academically but by the hope of reconnecting with her in the future.

As the last exam approached and the project submission loomed, he felt a mixture of anxiety and exhilaration. College was ending, but his feelings for her felt like a new beginning, a chapter yet to be written. He knew that no matter where life took him next, he would carry her memory with him—a beautiful reminder of a connection that sparked within him and gave him the courage to embrace his feelings.

With each passing day, the anticipation grew. He was ready to embark on the next part of his journey, one that he hoped would eventually lead him back to her.

19

A Twist of Fate

After graduation, Sai found himself in a familiar yet daunting situation—waiting for calls from companies where he had applied. Days turned into weeks, and as the silence stretched on, his confidence began to wane. Each time his phone buzzed, he would leap with anticipation, only to be met with disappointment when it was just a spam message or a notification from a social media app. The excitement of graduation faded, replaced by uncertainty and self-doubt.

Feeling the weight of stagnation pressing down on him, Sai realized he had to step out of his comfort zone. He packed his bags and made the bold decision to move to the city where he hoped to find better opportunities. Staying at his friend's place, he immersed himself in the job search. Every morning, he updated his resume, scoured job portals, and reached out to connections in hopes of landing interviews.

His efforts bore fruit when, after several weeks of searching, he received a call inviting him for an interview at a reputable company. The second interview turned out to be a turning point; he managed to impress the panel with his knowledge and enthusiasm, and he was offered the position on the spot. A rush of relief and excitement coursed through him as he accepted the offer. He returned home to pack his belongings, ready to start this new chapter of his life.

Once he settled into the new city, Sai dedicated himself to excelling in his role. The initial thrill of learning new things and meeting new people fueled his determination. He worked diligently, absorbing knowledge like a sponge, eager to prove himself. As the months flew by, his efforts began to pay off; he gained recognition for his hard work and commitment.

But as time went on, a familiar sense of monotony crept in. After a year, Sai found himself feeling bored and unfulfilled. One sunny afternoon, feeling overwhelmed by the routine, he decided to take a break. He headed to the beach, hoping the sound of crashing waves and the salty breeze would refresh his spirit.

Sitting on the soft sand, he gazed out at the endless sea, lost in thought. The beauty of the ocean stirred something within him—a longing for connection, a yearning for the moments he had shared with others. With a hint of nostalgia, he pulled out his phone and snapped a photo of the serene landscape, posting it to his Instagram story. As he began scrolling through his feed, he felt a sense of calm wash over him.

As he flipped through pictures, he came across several friend suggestions. One face stood out, sending his heart racing—a girl with familiar features and a warm smile. He couldn't believe his eyes. It was her, the girl he had met years ago during the college competition. The memories flooded back, igniting feelings he thought he had buried under the weight of his busy life.

Curiosity piqued, he clicked on her profile, and a wave of happiness washed over him. There, in her photos, he saw the vibrancy and joy that had drawn him to her in the first place. To his astonishment, he noticed that they had mutual friends—his colleagues from the office. His heart raced as he finally learned her name: Dee.

A spark of excitement ignited within him, and he decided to dig deeper. He switched to LinkedIn and searched for her name. His fingers danced over the keyboard as he typed. When her profile popped up, his eyes widened in disbelief. She had joined the same company a year after him, coincidentally becoming part of the same department he worked with. The realization that she was just a few desks away sent a thrill down his spine.

The world suddenly felt smaller and brighter, filled with possibilities. The chance of reconnecting with her, of discovering the path their lives had taken since that fateful competition, sent his heart racing with anticipation. He didn't expect to find her here, in the same office, after all this time.

Sai couldn't help but smile at the thought of what this could mean for him. Maybe he would finally get the opportunity to express his feelings, to bridge the gap between them that had lingered for so long. A sense of determination ignited within him; he knew he had to reach out, to rekindle that connection.

As he left the beach, the sunset painted the sky in shades of orange and pink, reflecting the newfound hope in his heart. He felt a surge of energy as he made his way home, eager to see where this unexpected twist of fate would lead him next.

20

The Long-Awaited Moment

Sai couldn't contain his excitement as the weekend passed. Thoughts of Dee consumed his mind, swirling like leaves caught in a gentle autumn breeze. It had been nearly two years since they had crossed paths, and now, fate had brought them to the same office. He envisioned how she might look after all this time—would her smile still light up the room? Would she still have that infectious laughter that echoed in his heart?

The anticipation of seeing her again sent butterflies fluttering wildly in his stomach. He imagined her walking into the office, her hair cascading over her shoulders like a waterfall of silk. He could picture the way her eyes sparkled with mischief, and how her laughter had a way of making even the dullest days feel brighter. All weekend, he found himself lost in memories of their brief encounters, replaying every moment and every smile in his mind.

Finally, Monday dawned, and with it came a surge of nervous energy. Sai arrived at the office early, his heart racing as he scanned the entrance, hoping to catch a glimpse of her. The familiar hustle and bustle of the workplace faded into the background as he focused solely on the door, willing her to walk through it.

But as the minutes turned into hours, disappointment began to creep in. He walked the hallways, peering into every meeting room and common area, yet she remained elusive. Where could she be? Did she have a different schedule? As the clock ticked away, he felt a knot tighten in his stomach.

In a moment of distraction, he decided to take a break and went to the printer to collect some documents. As he waited, he absently glanced around the office, still hoping to spot her. And then, there she was.

In a quiet corner, standing gracefully, Dee was engaged in conversation with a colleague. A wave of disbelief washed over him. She looked even more beautiful than he remembered. Her hair, now longer and slightly tousled, framed her face perfectly, accentuating her delicate features. She wore a light blue blouse that complemented her complexion, the fabric draping elegantly over her figure. The sunlight streaming through the window highlighted her hair, giving it a golden halo effect, making her look ethereal.

Sai stood frozen for a moment, captivated by the sight of her. Her laughter floated through the air like music, a sound he had missed more than he realized. The way she smiled, her eyes sparkling with warmth and genuine joy, made his heart race. It was as if time had stood still, and the world around him faded into oblivion.

He took a deep breath, trying to steady himself. This was the moment he had been waiting for, and yet, a sense of hesitation washed over him. How could he approach her without feeling like a fool? He knew he had to make an effort, to find a way to establish a connection.

As he mustered the courage to walk toward her, he couldn't help but admire the way she carried herself with grace and poise. Her confidence was magnetic, drawing people in like moths to a flame. In that instant, he felt a surge of determination. He would not let this opportunity slip away.

Over the next few days, Sai made it a point to observe her whenever he could. He would casually walk through the corridors, his heart racing each time he caught a glimpse of her, whether she was deep in conversation with colleagues in the cafeteria or laughing with friends by the coffee machine. She seemed to light up every room she entered, her presence igniting a spark in the air.

He found himself hanging around the cafeteria during lunch hours, trying to be near her, to steal glances of her radiant smile. Each time their eyes met, even if for a brief moment, it felt like an electric jolt, igniting hope within him. It was a silent acknowledgment, a connection that only he could understand.

In the days that followed, Sai resolved to be brave. He couldn't let fear hold him back any longer. If he was going to find a way to express his feelings, he needed to take that first step. He had to find a way to talk to her, to bridge the gap that time and circumstance had created.

As he navigated through his day-to-day tasks, the thought of Dee lingered in the back of his mind like a sweet melody, urging him to make his move. He felt invigorated by the possibilities, and with each passing moment, he became more determined to turn those fleeting glances into meaningful conversations.

Deep down, he knew he had to seize the moment. With newfound resolve, Sai prepared to confront his feelings, ready to take the plunge into the unknown—because he believed that this time, he wouldn't let fear dictate his heart.

21

The Unseen Remedy

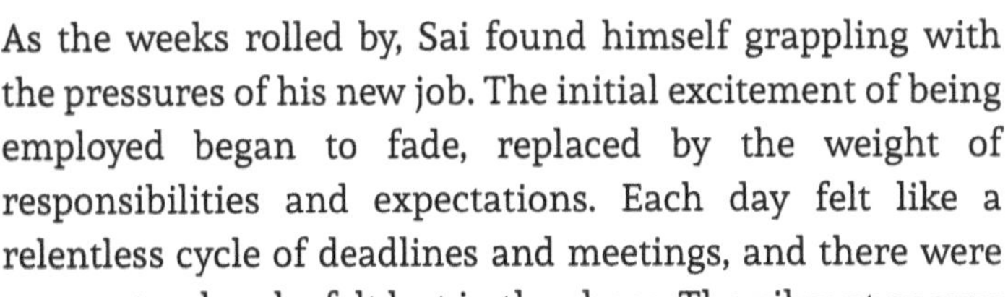

As the weeks rolled by, Sai found himself grappling with the pressures of his new job. The initial excitement of being employed began to fade, replaced by the weight of responsibilities and expectations. Each day felt like a relentless cycle of deadlines and meetings, and there were moments when he felt lost in the chaos. The vibrant energy of his college days now felt like a distant memory, and the loneliness crept in like a shadow.

Whenever he faced challenges, whether it was a tough project or a missed deadline, he would often retreat to the quiet corners of his mind, battling feelings of discouragement. Yet, amidst the darkness, one light shone brightly—Dee. Just the thought of her had the power to lift his spirits.

Whenever he felt low, he would find himself instinctively reaching for his phone, scrolling through his Instagram feed until her name appeared. Her posts were like a balm for his soul. A snapshot of her smiling face, a candid moment captured during a day out, or even a simple story of her enjoying a cup of coffee—each image served as a reminder of the warmth she brought into his life.

Her first meeting had left a lasting impression on him, and now, looking at her photos felt like a nostalgic embrace. She was the same girl who had unknowingly brightened his world during that college competition. Her laughter, her carefree spirit—it all resonated with him, reminding him of the connection they had shared, even if only for a brief moment.

After sending her requests on Instagram and LinkedIn, Sai felt a rush of exhilaration when she accepted them. When he saw the notification pop up, a smile broke across his face. It felt like a small victory, a sign that maybe, just maybe, she remembered him too. Every new post she shared brought him joy, a glimmer of happiness in the otherwise mundane routine of his days. He relished each notification, eager to see what she was up to, as if her life were a story he couldn't put down.

Yet, there were days when she wouldn't come into the office. On those days, he would find himself waiting anxiously for her posts, like a child waiting for the arrival of a favorite toy. He would sit alone in his room, scrolling through her Instagram stories, each one a window into her life that made him feel connected, even from a distance.

During those moments of solitude, he would often open her profile, revisiting her old posts—the ones where she radiated happiness, showcasing adventures, laughter, and the beauty of everyday life. Each picture was like a time capsule, allowing him to step into the warmth of her world. No matter the difficulties he faced—be it a demanding project or the stress of adapting to a new environment—seeing her brought a sense of comfort that was hard to describe.

Sai often thought about approaching her, about expressing the feelings that had grown within him like wildflowers in a forgotten garden. But there was always a nagging fear holding him back. What if she didn't feel the same? What if he misread their connection? The thought of losing what little he had—the comfort of her presence from afar—terrified him.

It was a constant battle between desire and fear. He cherished the comfort she provided in his life without even knowing it. Dee had unknowingly become his remedy for loneliness, a source of inspiration and strength.

As he navigated the highs and lows of his daily life, he often found himself smiling at his phone, feeling that familiar flutter in his chest whenever he saw her name pop up on his screen. She was a ray of sunshine in his otherwise gray world, a beautiful reminder that even amid struggles, there could be moments of joy.

But with each passing day, the longing to speak to her grew stronger. He yearned to know her, to share his thoughts and dreams, to create new memories together. However, the fear of rejection loomed large, a shadow that dampened his courage. For now, he resolved to enjoy the happiness she brought him from afar, holding onto the hope that one day he would find the right moment to approach her—when the stars aligned, and the fear subsided.

Until then, he would remain in the comfort of her digital presence, letting her unknowingly light the way through the challenges life threw at him.

22

The Proposal

The office was quiet that afternoon, the kind of calm that comes after the peak of a busy week. Sai sat at his desk, lost in thought as his fingers lazily tapped at his keyboard. He glanced at the clock every few minutes, not because he was in a hurry to leave, but because his mind kept drifting to Dee. She was someone he had thought about for far too long now, longer than he cared to admit. It had been years since that first fleeting moment during a college competition, but somehow, their paths had crossed again, here at the same office.

He hadn't spoken to her much beyond the usual pleasantries, but just seeing her around, exchanging polite smiles, felt like something special. Even though he knew she had no memory of him from that day long ago, for Sai, her presence was enough to stir up all the feelings he had buried over time.

Suddenly, the soft sound of approaching footsteps pulled him out of his thoughts. He looked up, and there she was—Dee, standing in front of his desk with a gentle smile, though there was something different about her today. Her usual confident demeanor was replaced with a hint of nervousness, as if she had something important to say but wasn't quite sure how to begin. She hesitated, tucking a loose strand of hair behind her ear before speaking.

"Hey, Sai," Dee said, her voice soft yet steady, "Do you have a moment? I was hoping we could talk."

Sai felt his heart skip a beat, the suddenness of her request making his pulse quicken. What could this be about? He had no idea, but the curious tone in her voice made him both anxious and intrigued.

"Yeah, sure. What's up?" he responded, trying to keep his voice as casual as possible, though he could feel the flurry of emotions building inside him.

"Can we go somewhere a bit more private? Maybe the staircase?" Dee asked, her eyes briefly meeting his before looking away, as if to shield whatever emotions were hiding behind them.

Sai nodded without saying a word, feeling a mix of anticipation and nervousness flood through him. He stood up from his desk and followed her through the office corridors. They walked in silence, the only sound being the faint rustle of papers and the occasional hum of printers in the background. The staircase was quiet, secluded—just the two of them, away from the prying eyes of their colleagues.

As they reached the steps, Dee sat down on one of the lower steps, her posture slightly slouched, indicating a mix of unease and determination. Sai, unsure of where to sit, hesitated before choosing a step just below hers. The proximity between them felt electrifying, though neither of them spoke for a few moments. It was a silence that held weight, as if both were waiting for the other to break it.

Dee glanced at Sai, and though her smile was small, it was sincere. "Actually... can you come sit on the same step as me?" she asked with a shy laugh, gesturing beside her.

Sai felt a surge of warmth at her request, and without hesitation, he moved up a step to sit next to her. Their shoulders brushed slightly, sending a spark of emotion through him that he struggled to contain. This closeness, after all this time, felt surreal. He had admired her from afar for so long, never daring to hope for something like this. He could see her from this angle—the soft curve of her cheek, the way her eyelashes fluttered nervously, the light reflecting off the necklace she wore around her neck. She was beautiful, more beautiful than he had ever let himself imagine. And here they were, closer than they'd ever been before.

Dee shifted slightly, her hands resting on her lap as she gathered the courage to speak. "I've been wanting to tell you something for a while now, but I wasn't sure how," she began, her voice quieter than before. "We've worked together for two years, and though we don't interact much, I've seen you around. And… I don't know when it happened, but I started to like you. A lot. It's not just a crush. I think I've fallen in love with you, Sai."

Her words hit him like a wave. Sai sat frozen, his heart pounding in his chest. This was the moment he had never thought would come—the girl he had admired for so long, the one who had unknowingly given him hope, was confessing her feelings to him. He opened his mouth to respond, but the words didn't come out. How could he possibly explain everything he had felt for her, all these years of silent admiration?

After a deep breath, he found his voice. "Dee, there's something I need to tell you too." He paused, his thoughts racing as he tried to put into words what had been in his heart for so long. "I saw you years ago, at a college competition. It was my first time at an event like that, and I was feeling pretty low. But then... I saw you. Just seeing you made everything feel better. Since that day, I haven't been able to stop thinking about you."

Dee's eyes widened, surprise flickering across her face. "You saw me back then? I had no idea."

Sai nodded, the weight of his confession lifting from his shoulders. "I did. And then, when I found out you were working here, it felt like fate. Like we were meant to meet again."

For a moment, there was silence between them, as Dee took in his words. Sai could feel the tension in the air, a mix of relief and anticipation. He watched as Dee's expression softened, her lips curling into a small, unsure smile.

"Does that mean... you feel the same way?" Dee asked, her voice barely audible, yet filled with hope.

Sai looked at her, his heart full of emotions he had tried to suppress for so long. "I think I always have."

They sat there, the weight of their confessions hanging between them like a fragile thread. Dee, still blushing from the intensity of the moment, let out a soft laugh, breaking the tension. "This feels so surreal," she said, glancing down at her hands. "I never expected you to have such a story."

Sai smiled too, feeling a sense of lightness that he hadn't experienced in a long time. "Neither did I. But here we are."

Before either of them could say anything else, Dee stood up suddenly, her nervousness replaced with excitement. "Let's get out of here," she said with a grin, her eyes sparkling. "Come on, let's go for a ride."

Sai, still reeling from everything that had just happened, followed her without hesitation. As they walked out of the building together, he couldn't help but marvel at how quickly things had changed. The girl he had once only admired from afar was now beside him, and they were about to embark on something new—something real.

The ride through the city was exhilarating, the cool breeze whipping through their hair as they sped through the streets. It was a moment of freedom, of possibilities, and for the first time in a long while, Sai felt at peace. They stopped at a cozy little café, ordering coffee and sitting in a corner, talking about everything and nothing.

This wasn't a dream—it was real.

As the evening came to a close, they rode back to the office, the sun setting behind them, casting a golden glow over the city. Just before they parted ways, Dee turned to him, her face glowing with warmth.

"Thank you for today," she whispered, her smile soft and sincere. Then, in a moment of spontaneity, she leaned in and gave Sai a quick, warm hug, leaving him standing there, speechless.

And just as he was about to respond, his alarm blared. Sai sat up in his bed, the morning sun streaming through his window. He blinked, confused and disoriented, the vividness of the dream still clinging to him.

It had all been a dream.

But even as reality set in, Sai couldn't help but feel a strange sense of hope. He had seen Dee in the office yesterday, and now, with the possibility of making this dream a reality, he knew that things might be about to change.

Sai lay in bed, sunlight filtering through the curtains as he replayed the dream in his mind. The conversation with Dee on the staircase, her confession, their coffee ride—it had all felt so real. But now, as he sat up, the reality of the office awaited him. What was the dream trying to tell him?

He sighed, glancing at the clock. It was almost time to head to work. The dream had left him feeling restless, but also hopeful. Could it be a sign? He was going to see Dee today, just like every other day—but today felt different.

Walking into the office that morning, Sai's eyes instinctively searched for her. Dee wasn't at her desk yet, and the office buzzed with the usual energy of a new workday. His mind was still tangled in the emotions from the dream, but he tried to shake them off. He needed to focus on his tasks for the day, but thoughts of Dee kept pulling him away.

After settling at his desk, Sai forced himself to focus on the project deadline looming over him. The screen in front of him displayed lines of code, but his mind drifted. He found himself glancing towards the entrance, waiting for the moment when Dee would walk in.

And then she did. Dee, wearing a bright yellow salwar, the same color she wore in the dream. His breath caught for a moment. Could it be a coincidence? The dream was still fresh in his mind, and seeing her like this felt almost surreal. She walked past, unaware of his gaze, and settled at her desk with her usual grace.

Sai tried to focus on work, but his thoughts kept drifting back to the dream. How strange it felt—years after that fleeting encounter at the college competition, they were now working side by side. Neither of them had mentioned the past, but for Sai, it had always lingered in the background.

As the hours passed, the routine of the office began to ground him. Meetings, emails, and deadlines filled his day, but every now and then, he would catch himself glancing at Dee. She seemed busy, engrossed in her own tasks. The dream had stirred something in him—hope, maybe, or even a quiet longing—but he knew better than to rush things.

During lunch, Sai sat with his colleagues, making small talk, but his mind was elsewhere. He thought about the future, about how his life had changed over the years. The job had given him stability, but something still felt incomplete. Perhaps it was the unresolved feelings for Dee that made him feel this way.

As the day went on, Dee remained a quiet presence, focused on her work. The connection between them, though unspoken, felt stronger than before. The dream had awakened something in him—an awareness that maybe, just maybe, their paths were crossing again for a reason.

When the workday ended, Sai felt a strange mix of relief and anticipation. He packed up his things, ready to head home, but his mind lingered on Dee. The dream, her confession, their closeness—it all felt like a possibility now, something he hadn't dared to hope for before.

As he left the office, the cool evening air hit him, and he found himself smiling. He didn't know what the future held, but for the first time in a long while, he felt ready for it. Maybe it wasn't a dream after all. Maybe it was a sign of something real, something waiting to unfold.

23

The Moment of Truth

Months had passed since that pivotal dream on the staircase. The days turned into weeks, and the weeks into months, as they continued to work alongside each other in the bustling office. They were part of a team that had taken on a significant project, one that was crucial for the company's upcoming product launch. The collaboration had brought them closer, creating a bond that was both professional and personal.

Finally, after weeks of late nights and shared laughter, the project was nearing completion. To celebrate their hard work, the team organized an outing—a chance to unwind and reflect on their achievements. As the day approached, excitement buzzed in the air. But for him, there was an undercurrent of anxiety, too.

As they gathered at the venue, the atmosphere was lively. Colleagues shared stories, laughed over drinks, and reflected on the long hours they had put in. He watched Dee as she animatedly spoke with a group of coworkers, her laughter ringing like music. He felt a rush of warmth each time he glanced her way, but the little fear in his heart remained.

After a while, the team settled into a circle, sharing their experiences from the project. As the evening wore on, he felt a shift in his gut, a tug of urgency. This was his chance—the moment he had been waiting for. But what if he ruined everything?

Finally, the moment arrived when the circle shifted to her, and she spoke about the importance of teamwork, gratitude for the project, and how it had taught her so much. The words hung in the air, and his heart raced as he decided to take the leap.

"Dee," he started, his voice steady despite the pounding in his chest, "I've been wanting to ask you something."

She turned to him, her eyes sparkling with curiosity. "What is it?"

He hesitated for a moment, the weight of his question pressing on him. Thoughts raced through his mind, filled with the fear of what revealing his feelings might mean for their fragile connection. Taking a deep breath, he gathered his courage and forged ahead.

"What was your first love like?"

The question hung in the air, the room fading away as he focused solely on her. Dee's expression changed, a hint of surprise mingled with contemplation.

After a moment, she smiled softly, and he felt a flicker of hope. "Well, it was complicated, really," she began, her voice gentle yet distant as if she were revisiting a cherished memory. "He was someone I admired from afar, a quiet boy who always seemed to be lost in his own world. I remember the way he smiled when he thought no one was watching, how his laughter felt like sunshine breaking through a cloudy day. I was drawn to him in a way I couldn't explain."

Her gaze drifted, lost in thought. "We never really connected, but he taught me a lot about myself. It was more about the experience than the person, I think. I learned what it meant to care for someone, even if it was from a distance. Those moments of longing, of imagining what could have been, shaped how I view relationships now."

As she spoke, he realized that the pieces of her story felt familiar—stories he had overheard from others, fragments that suddenly clicked into place. And with every detail she shared, he felt a strange sense of calm wash over him.

The conversation continued, and he learned more about her past—stories that echoed his own feelings of uncertainty and hope. They laughed together, reminiscing about moments that seemed so distant yet so alive in their hearts.

By the end of the night, he felt lighter. Though he hadn't revealed his own feelings, he understood her in a new way. The fear that had held him back transformed into gratitude. They had shared this moment, this understanding, and perhaps that was enough for now.

As they all prepared to leave, he caught her eye one last time. Dee smiled at him, a knowing look that made his heart race once more. They had forged a connection through the uncertainty, and for him, that was just the beginning.

Stepping out into the night, he felt a surge of hope. No matter where the journey led, they had both embarked on something meaningful, and he was ready to see where it would take them next.